T0083500

Aosenla's Story

Aosenla's Story

TEMSULA AO

ZUBAAN
128 B Shahpur Jat, 1st floor
NEW DELHI 110 049
Email: contact@zubaanbooks.com
Website: www.zubaanbooks.com

First published by Zubaan Publishers Pvt. Ltd 2017

10 9 8 7 6 5 4 3 2 1

ISBN 978 93 84757 98 4

Zubaan is an independent feminist publishing house based in New Delhi with a strong academic and general list. It was set up as an imprint of India's first feminist publishing house, Kali for Women, and carries forward Kali's tradition of publishing world quality books to high editorial and production standards. *Zubaan* means tongue, voice, language, speech in Hindustani. Zubaan publishes in the areas of the humanities, social sciences, as well as in fiction, general non-fiction, and books for children and young adults under its Young Zubaan imprint.

Typeset in Adobe Garamond 11/14 by Jojy Philip, New Delhi 110 015
Printed and bound at Raj Press, R-3 Inderpuri, New Delhi 110 012

Freeing oneself was one thing:
claiming ownership of that freed self was another.

Toni Morrison
(*Beloved*, p. 95. Picador)

For my daughters
Jungmayangla
Imtinungla
Sungtiyenla

1

It was a typical summer afternoon, turning into another, predictable, oppressive evening. The atmosphere was still heavy with the accumulated heat of the day. The anticipated coolness of dusk was some indeterminate distance away. Amidst the gathering interplay of fading light and threatening darkness, a first-time visitor could make out the outlines of a big estate, which appeared to be gradually coming to life. The two houses within were still visible: the big one with its imposing façade and the smaller one, almost demure, in its country-cottage sereneness. A few disjointed sounds of water running from taps, garbled human voices, and the clatter of utensils wafted out from the house. In the verandah of the smaller house, a lone figure sat in the gathering dusk, quiet, seemingly indifferent to the sounds and smells of the darkening day.

The woman sat, listening with only half an ear to the racket her children and their friends were making in the grounds adjacent to their grandfather's sprawling compound. For some time now, she had wanted to tell the maid that it was time to bathe and prepare them for the evening's rituals. But somehow she remained quiet, as if she lacked the will or energy to do anything. Her gaze drifted towards the big house, the house that had symbolized authority and domination over her life ever since she had entered it as a daughter-in-law. She wondered how an inanimate object like a house could wield so much power. Was it the structure, which tended to dwarf the smaller one that she could at least call her own? Or was it the aura of the people who lived in the big house, who seemed so sure of themselves, and at every given opportunity tried to remind her of her origins and her place in life? A summons to the big house always made her cringe; had she done anything to displease the gods residing there? Or would she receive new diktats about an impending family event? As she continued to gaze at the formidable structure, she willed her attention back to the verandah of the smaller house where she was sitting; this had been her 'home' since she got married. Within these walls, she grudgingly admitted, she had enjoyed at least a certain amount of freedom and even an occasional happy moment. But once she stepped outside its perimeter, she was no longer her own self; she was the wife of a rich man and the daughter-in-law of an influential family. She no longer had an independent identity.

As she turned her attention once again to the big compound, she could see her mother-in-law, big in size as well as in pride, ordering the gardener and an assortment of servants to restore the landscape to its original condition, before the children had created the mess. An older man, and the gardener were trying to say something in reply to a command, 'Otsu, Otsu, Obou said…' But before the gardner could say anything further, the matriarch shouted back at him, 'Never mind what the old man said, do as I told you', and haughtily walked into the house, leaving him dumbstruck and the other servants giggling at his discomfiture. As if to remind them of what they were supposed to be doing, there came the strident voice of the matriarch shouting at the cook over something he had or had not done. Aosenla took in the various nuances of the domestic drama and marvelled at the negative energy of this formidable woman. She was glad that she was not directly under her command in these daily routines, thanks to the age-old custom that required the sons to set up a separate household after marriage. The problem was that their new home was within the big estate, and therefore the old couple still managed to dominate the new household in more ways than Aosenla liked. But she had to live with this semi-independence and was ever careful to avoid any direct contact or conflict with people in the big house, especially her mother-in-law.

She continued to sit there fanning herself with the big wedding invitation card that had been delivered earlier in the day. She had looked at the ornate gold letters announcing the marriage of the son of the town's uncrowned king, an immensely wealthy and powerful business tycoon. But she did not recognize the girl's name immediately and sat there trying to place her by the names of her parents. Then she recalled a bit of gossip she had heard a few weeks ago: the bride-to-be was the daughter of a minor functionary in the Deputy Commissioner's office, and she was a teacher in one of the lower primary schools in town. She also remembered what the town gossip had said to her sister-in-law, 'The boy's parents are saying that she will not be allowed keep her job once they are married.' Recalling these bits of gossip, and also the disparity in the social standing of the families, it became apparent to her, as it would to anybody else, that this marriage was indeed one of convenience. Moreover, the boy was notorious for his escapades, especially with girls, and hence perhaps the choice of this simple girl from a humble background who would not dare protest, should he continue with his old ways even after marriage. She felt strangely disturbed by these thoughts and continued fanning herself absent-mindedly though the evening was getting cooler by the minute.

As though a trigger had been set off somewhere deep in her mind, her thoughts went back to her own marriage so many summers ago. Just as the marriage of convenience that was going to take place in a week's time, hers too had been similar. The faithful maid recognized that her mistress was in one of her moods and she tactfully steered the children away to give her time to compose herself. Aosenla's mood that evening seemed to overwhelm her more than usual, so the maid supervised the bath and fed the children an early meal and withdrew to her own quarters. The woman continued to sit there amidst the gathering gloom while distant lights could be seen in other houses circling the estate. When a servant put on the verandah lights, she tersely told him to switch off the 'damn' things. She wanted to remain within the circle of darkness.

To be in the shadows forever: how comforting that would be. To not have to face the disapproving eyes of her mother-in-law whom she had 'failed' by giving birth only to girls. To ignore her husband's philandering ways and to pretend to the world that her marriage was fine had somehow become the main purpose of her life now. Stay here forever, urged her timid self, let the servants manage the household. Stay in, said her voiceless self, unable to give vent to the frustrations of a hapless life. It was as if she could be herself only in the protective isolation of darkness, and so she allowed herself the luxury of soaking in the deepening shadows of the evening.

She remembered very clearly that it was during her second year in college that her dream world had fallen apart. She had won a scholarship to pursue further studies, but as her retired father could not afford to pay the hostel fees in a bigger town, she had to be content with going to the local college. For her, that had been good enough, because until the scholarship from the government was confirmed, there was no hope of her ever going to any college. She enjoyed the new environment; surprisingly, there were many good teachers who encouraged the students and helped them out with books and other things they needed. Aosenla felt that she was gaining a lot of self-confidence and was also doing well in her studies. Her good looks and modest behaviour earned the admiration of her fellow students. She began to dream of a life beyond college; she would try to earn another scholarship and go out to do her post-graduate degree and find a decent job. She would look after her ageing parents and make them proud of her. She was motivated to make something of her life, a life that had hitherto always been restricted by the compulsions of poverty and uncertainty about the future.

The first year seemed to have simply flown by, taking with it her initial awkwardness in the company of more privileged students. She was beginning to feel at home in the college, with intellectual stimulation from the teachers and the goodwill of her fellow students. And this new sensation added a certain glow to her personality. The sad demeanour was gone; she became livelier and began to take part in extra-curricular activities. Faculty and students alike noticed the subtle changes in her and began to look upon her transformation with interest and growing admiration. Aosenla also began to dream of a future where she would create a new world for herself and her family and prove that, given the opportunity, even a supposedly ordinary person could achieve great things. Being among her peers, both rich and poor alike, was an eye-opener for Aosenla; she began to realize that there was a level-playing field where merit counted.

This blissful state of affairs was, however, short-lived. One evening, her mother came into her room looking very serious. It was clear that she was upset over something, and after much cajoling she tearfully blurted out that Aosenla was going to be married the next month. The girl felt stricken, as if felled by a painful physical blow. Nothing could have been further from her mind; she protested that she had just started her second year of college; there were two more years before she graduated. And, she added, she was determined to do her post-graduation from a good university. The mother was weeping by now at her daughter's distress. Between sobs, she told Aosenla that her father had refused to listen to her and that he wished her to stay at home from now on until the marriage. Aosenla flew into a rage, shouting, 'Wish! Does he wish that I stop living? What about my wishes? Has anyone asked me if I want to get married to a man I have not even seen?' The mother was barely literate but she had noticed the subtle changes in her daughter ever since she joined college. She had rejoiced secretly that her daughter was now so obviously happy. She did not need any education to tell her this.

But now the father's 'wish' cast a pall of gloom on the household and left the mother caught between loyalty to her husband and sympathy for her daughter. Unlike Aosenla, her mother viewed her father's motivation as genuinely reasonable; which father could resist an offer like this? But at the same time, unlike the father who seemed to be blind and deaf to his daughter's protestations, the mother understood her daughter's agony and yet was unable to express her concern openly. If Aosenla felt frustrated by the father's will, the mother's plight was worse. In spite of her sympathy for her daughter, she had to align herself with her husband because she was brought up to believe that it was the bounden duty of a wife to support her husband, especially in a situation like this. The mother was at first afraid to tell her husband how the daughter had reacted, and merely said, 'Don't worry, she'll come round'. The father was uneasy but held his peace. Aosenla stayed home from college for two days, and the father thought that she was 'coming round' just as his wife had reported. What he did not know was that his daughter had secretly decided to leave on the third day, when her father usually went to a friend's house for a smoke and some local gossip. But it was not to be, because just as she finished dressing and was about to step out through the bathroom door, she heard her mother calling out to her. She had no alternative but to respond to her summons. As she walked to the kitchen where her mother stood waiting for her, she saw her father sitting with his cronies in the small drawing room and her heart sank.

When her mother saw her in outdoor clothes, she immediately guessed what her daughter had planned to do. She looked at her hard, and hissed, 'Don't try to do anything foolish,' and then instantly raising her voice so that it would carry to her husband, she said, 'O Asen, your father is having his session in our house today; go make some snacks and good masala tea for them.' Aosenla ran back to her room to change and returned to the kitchen. She began to prepare the tea and snacks, but she rattled the dishes so much that her mother had to come and caution her not to provoke her father who would obviously understand why she was behaving in this manner. When the tea and snacks were ready, Aosenla called her mother and told her to serve them, as she was feeling a bit dizzy. Without a word, the mother picked up the tray and went into the drawing room where the men were laughing loudly over something. On the surface, things looked normal. But there was a palpable tension that affected everyone in the family. From that day on, Aosenla stayed cooped up in her room most of the day and night, coming out to eat and walk around the house only when her father was away. The brothers became more taciturn and the mother withdrew further into herself.

This state of affairs however could not be kept hidden for long from the relatives, and there was great consternation in her extended family. They were at first baffled: how could the parents jeopardize the prospects of an excellent match like this by giving in to the tantrums of a selfish girl? They berated the parents for being too lenient with their children, especially the daughter. But how could the parents convince this headstrong girl that this was being done to secure her future? She simply refused to listen to the mother's pleas, saying that she wanted to continue with her studies. The father fumed, 'What studies? Will her degree bring a groom such as this one?' Turning to his wife, he thundered, 'Woman, go knock some sense into your daughter. I have accepted their offer, and the marriage must take place as planned. I should have never allowed her to go to college in the first place; it is all this strange learning that has addled her brain.' He delivered this ultimatum and stormed out of the house, returning only after everyone had retired for the night.

Barred from going to college, Aosenla spent most of her time in her room, often refusing to join the family at mealtimes. A marriage in the family is a time of celebration and joy; but for this humble family the prospect of this almost-forced marriage created an atmosphere of tension all around. Relatives, hearing of the girl's reaction to the proposal, did not want to get involved and curtailed their visits to the bare minimum. Instead of turning into a house of laughter and joy, this household seemed to be in mourning. The mother was the most affected as she was burdened with the task of convincing Aosenla to say yes to the proposal even though she secretly sympathized with her daughter. She saw what her husband refused to acknowledge: the boy was much older than her daughter; he also came from a prominent family, and she knew that Aosenla would always be at a disadvantage in such a household. Besides, the boy's sisters looked, dressed and behaved like 'memsahibs' who would certainly look down on this poor girl from nowhere. Yet, the onerous task of pushing her daughter into such a household became her 'responsibility' because it was her husband's 'wish'.

It was during this period of self-imposed isolation that, for the first time in her life, Aosenla realized what it meant to be a woman. She had never felt any discrimination in her parents' attitude towards her and the brothers. In fact, the brothers sometimes complained to their mother that the father was partial to their sister. For instance, when he had accompanied his boss to Calcutta once, he brought many presents for Aosenla and only some canvas shoes for them. They had both sulked for a week. It was true that she was clever and always stood first in her class. But while he made plans for the boys' college education, the father had secretly resolved that Aosenla would stop her studies after matriculation. It was not because he loved her less; his thinking was dictated by the fact she was a girl and had no need to study more because one day soon, she would be married off and would go away from this house to start life as a wife and daughter-in-law and set up another household. He had expected offers of marriage for his daughter to come pouring in once she had passed the matric exam, but when none came, and when his daughter managed to get a scholarship, he reluctantly allowed her to get admitted in the local college. He was now regretting his decision; he thought that the girl was behaving in this manner because she had tasted a bit of independence in college and was now threatening to defy his wishes. If Aosenla's opposition became public knowledge, he would not only lose face among his peers, but also earn the enmity of a prominent family in town. He could not afford this at the fag end of his life. Something had to be done and soon.

Staying away from college and shutting herself up in her room gave Aosenla time to introspect. She realized that she was destined to suffer the future that her father was now trying to foist on her. She seemed to have grown up within these two weeks of isolation, and began to look at her parents from a new perspective. She was convinced that if her mother were a stronger person, she would have tried to help her out. But she knew that she had always obeyed her husband meekly and this time too, though she would cry inwardly, she would not go against him openly and therefore would do nothing to help her daughter. Looking back on her growing years, Aosenla realized that all through, their lives had indeed revolved around what the father wished. He would determine which weddings and other gatherings they would attend, she even saw her mother once changing her clothes because her father did not approve of what she was wearing. As she sat ruminating on past events, she began to realize that her father's dealings with the boys were different. She could not actually pinpoint any specific incident, and therefore could not articulate what it was, but her father definitely seemed to be more at ease with her brothers. He would kick a football around with them when they were younger and sometimes even jump into the bath together with them, splashing water and laughing loudly. Sitting hunched up and sulking in her room, she remembered those moments of exclusion during her childhood and began to question this unapproachable side of her father's personality for the first time.

For a long time, she searched for a word that would define her relationship with her father. Ever since that night, when she was told that she had to stop going to college and was to be married, she had begun to resent him. She ranted in the presence of her mother that he was old-fashioned, insensitive and did not love her at all. Otherwise, she claimed, he would not have accepted the offer of marriage to a much older man, no matter how rich or influential the family was. The mother would listen to her patiently and walk out of the room without saying a word. On some days, she would enter her daughter's room and announce with an obviously contrived gaiety that her father wanted them to go to a wedding in the town or a birthday party somewhere, and that Aosenla must be ready on time. But Aosenla remained unresponsive to all such indirect overtures from her father and would utter only a gruff 'no'. One day, as she was dozing off, she suddenly sat up in bed and began to talk to herself. 'Why doesn't he talk to me directly? Why doesn't he come to explain to me why he has accepted the offer? Why does he treat me like a guest in this house? Why is he so formal?' The moment she uttered the word 'formal', she knew for certain that it was the word that she had been searching for all this while. Her father was sheltering himself from her opposition to the marriage by creating a distance between them through this formality. But what she did not realize was that in their society, most fathers behaved in a similar manner with their daughters.

When she thought back, she had to admit that the distance must have been created some time after she attained puberty, though she had not realized it at the time. From constant interactions with her friends' families, Aosenla must have assumed that all fathers were like that with teenage daughters. She now remembered how she used to tell her mother about things she needed for school; she never communicated directly with her father. However, her brothers seemed to have direct access to their father; they did not go through their mother. Before this period of soul-searching, Aosenla had never felt the need to introspect about her relationship with her parents or her brothers. There were so many things she had taken for granted because the same equations seemed to be at work in every other family. But now it was different; she was at a crossroads in her life and she was compelled to re-examine her relationship with her father. Here was a man who she had practically worshipped since childhood and in whom she had implicit faith. She believed he could never be wrong and that he would always be there for her. But circumstances had proven her wrong; her father seemed to have changed into another person who now stood in direct opposition to her aspirations. She was confused and disturbed because now a strange kind of antagonism had begun to grow within her towards this person, who did not resemble the man she had called 'father' all her life. If not an enemy, Aosenla certainly considered him an adversary who had betrayed her trust.

For the first time in her young life, Aosenla discovered how differently men thought about things. When the brothers learnt of her refusal to get married, they casually asked her, 'Why are you being so silly? Sooner or later you have to get married, so why not now?' 'But I don't love him, and he is an old man,' Aosenla replied. They burst out laughing, 'Who is talking about love? We are talking about you getting married to a rich man from a good family. And he is not that old, look at mom and dad, dad is much older. That did not stop their marriage, did it?' Aosenla was shocked by their attitude; they did not seem to be bothered about her, while she adored them both, and would have taken up their cause if anyone had bullied or threatened them. She was hurt initially by their seemingly callous remarks but when she could not assign any bias or motive to their response, it finally dawned on her that they too were men, and they thought differently. The instant she realized the difference, her relationship with them changed. Whereas earlier, she could talk to them freely about anything, books, cinema or sometimes even girls they liked, now she began to realize that men were different from women not only physically but also mentally, emotionally and intellectually. So far she had ignored the differences, but she'd be more cautious and suspicious from now on. She did not realize it then, but from then on, Aosenla stepped into a different realm of existence as a woman.

2

The father, on the other hand, was growing more apprehensive; he knew how obstinate his daughter could be and if he did not send a formal word of acceptance to the boy's family soon, the marriage would be off, and his family would be in disgrace. Though it was the girl who was refusing the offer, one never knew what a rich and influential family would do to safeguard their prestige; they might turn around and say that the girl had been rejected by them because of some blemish in her character. And then, for no fault of hers, Aosenla would be stigmatized for life. He knew that a family like his would never be able to hold their heads high and everyone would eventually get to know the story. He became increasingly irritable, but he still hoped that she would see reason and would give her consent soon. So he invited his sisters and sisters-in-law to the house so that they could reason with Aosenla and persuade her to say yes. But the young girl seemed impervious to their advice and once, when the women persisted, went to the extent of saying that if her parents considered her a burden, she could look for an alternative to the problem: she would go someplace else and look for a job! When the father heard about this, he went into a panic and began to sneak liquor bottles into the house. He was a reformed alcoholic, and when the wife smelled the dreaded smell on his breath in spite of his attempts at hiding it, she realized how precariously her husband stood on the brink of a relapse because of Aosenla's obduracy. So she took matters into her own hands and sent word to her mother in the village, telling her about the crisis and the likelihood of the proposed marriage falling through. Her mother-in-law was dead, she knew her father-in-law's fiery temper and did not want her ploy to become public knowledge through his indiscretion. It might make matters worse. Her mother, however, was a shrewd old woman who would handle her granddaughter well.

When the grandmother received her daughter's letter telling her about the girl's reluctance to marry and her talk of going away from home, she dispatched an urgent message saying she wanted to meet her granddaughter. Aosenla was not aware of the communication between her mother and grandmother, and when the message reached her she was glad because it would mean that she could escape, even though for a short while, and she would not have to see her mother's defeated face every morning or her father's ragged behaviour. So she set out for the village. But when she reached the next day, she found that there was nothing in her grandmother's manner or behaviour to justify the urgency with which she had been summoned. Though her maternal aunts and uncles dropped in to greet her, except for exchanging inane pleasantries, none of them mentioned the impending marriage even once. However, elsewhere in the village, her cousins were already agog with this romantic offer that had come their 'educated' cousin's way. They also seemed to be privy to a secret kept from their cousin and were eagerly awaiting the imminent unfolding of the drama. Inwardly, they felt envious of her and said that her reluctance was mere playacting. That the young girl was not enthusiastic about the proposal had by now become common knowledge in the village, and different groups had different interpretations of the proposed match, and her peculiar reaction to the proposal. The patriarchs said that the boy's father was doing the right thing by seeking an alliance with the founding clan. Others pooh-poohed the idea and said that these days nobody cared about these traditional things; money and family position had become more important than lineage and prominence in village history, especially for those who lived in towns. So, they thought, the girl's family should grab this opportunity and marry her off without any delay; drag her to the altar if need be. As for the girl, they said that it was all that 'foreign' influence at school and college that had turned her head and that was why she was behaving in this silly manner. Higher studies indeed, they scoffed, once she got married and had babies, all that fancy talk would disappear.

Aosenla was becoming increasingly irritated at being cooped up in her grandmother's house. The afternoon seemed to drag on; the old woman had gone out for her daily meeting with her friends, telling her to relax and get some rest. Aosenla retired to the inner room with a slight headache and lay down on the cot. The events of the last two weeks were beginning to wear her down. The abrupt and undreamt-of announcement of her marriage made her feel as if she was caught in a sudden whirlwind. Though she did threaten to leave home, she knew that she would never do that to her mother who had always been protective of her. Only, in the present circumstance, the mother seemed as helpless as the daughter. She realized that this hastily arranged trip to see an allegedly ailing grandmother was a ruse and was obviously meant to apply some more pressure on her so that she would give in. But the trip to see an 'ailing' grandmother was turning out to be a farce because the grandmother was merrily gallivanting around the village leaving her to her own devices. She resented being treated this way and began to pace in the small room but, after a while, had to lie down on the small bed because of a nagging headache.

Plagued by many disturbing thoughts, she fell into a restless sleep and when she woke up, it was already dusk. Her grandmother had cooked the evening meal, and they sat down to an early dinner. Though she was not hungry at all, she ate a bit. The old woman saw the half-eaten meal but did not say anything. After some time, she told Aosenla that they were expected at her eldest maternal uncle's house. Aosenla did not ask her why but meekly followed her grandmother. However, when they reached the uncle's house, she was in for a big surprise: Bendangmeren, the groom-to-be, was sitting on the only decent chair near the central fireplace as if he was some visiting dignitary. She had not seen him at such close quarters before and was momentarily flustered by his presence, so she headed straight for the bamboo platform at the back of the house, where she was joined by her cousin who was doing her best to suppress her giggles. Though it was spring, the evening was becoming chilly and she was glad that she had carried a shawl with her. The sky was obscured by mist and the moonlight was faint. Only the glow from the kitchen fire provided a patch of light on a section of the platform. Her cousin tried to make conversation but she was in no mood for small talk. She was wondering what her fate was going to be, with the suitor sitting inside the house and everyone around him behaving as if he was a great benefactor. If she said no to his face, how would he react? What would happen to her family? What would she do, where would she go? It was one thing to protest in the safety of her own home but quite another in the presence of the one who was asking for her hand in marriage. She felt betrayed and cornered; she raged within herself at her grandmother who had so cunningly engineered this encounter and made her so vulnerable. But after the initial panic, she told herself to be firm and not yield her ground. After a while her grandmother came out to join her and told the cousin to go inside. She pulled Aosenla aside and whispered to her, 'Remember this will please your mother immensely because he is from her own clan. As for you, don't have any crazy ideas about yourself. A woman, no matter how educated or rich or well-placed, needs the protection of a man all her life. A man may be blind or lame or ugly, but he is superior because he is a man and we are women and helpless. No matter what, do not commit the mistake of saying no. You owe a duty to all of us.' So saying, she went out of the house leaving Aosenla alone on the creaky platform.

Aosenla did not know what she should do. Should she follow her grandmother, go inside the house or call her cousin back to the platform? Why had the old woman left her here? She looked around, it was dark everywhere and the faint moonlight strangely enhanced the darkness around her. She decided that it was absurd for her to be stranded in the eerie darkness and was about to go inside. But to her horror, she saw the man coming towards her and, in the faint light of the fire inside the house, she saw that he had a slight smile on his face. She was petrified. He looked much older, had a supercilious air about him and he called out to someone to bring out the chair he was sitting on. Aosenla stood as if rooted to the spot. He called out once again, and a stool was brought for her. She sat reluctantly. He did not say anything for a while, but Aosenla felt that he was looking at her intently, though she wondered if he could see anything at all in the enveloping darkness surrounding them. At last, he opened his mouth and asked her, 'Why are you so unwilling to marry me?' For a face-to-face meeting for the first time, she considered these words to be extremely rude and thought him uncouth in the extreme. She was also taken aback by the directness and haughty tone of the question; it was almost accusatory, as if she had committed an offence. For quite some time she remained silent. When he repeated the question, she replied, 'I want to study further,' and almost as an afterthought, she added, 'and besides I am too young to get married now.' Her answer caught him off-guard, but he composed himself and continued, 'Why are you being so obstinate? Everyone in our families wants us to get married, except you. I want to marry you because I already like you.' Absentmindedly she thought, 'He said "like" and not "love"'.

She remained mute because she could not think of any rejoinder to his comment; all that she wanted to do at that moment was to get away from the overwhelming compulsion of having to say 'yes'. It was turning out to be a contest of wills, and she realized that she was beginning to lose some of the vehemence of her initial opposition. She could not say what was causing this dangerous weakening of her will and seeming withdrawal from the contest. Was it the presence of this man who loomed so large on her horizon? Was it her sense of family loyalty as demanded by her grandmother? It became increasingly clear to her that if she was to avoid being caught in the tactical manoeuvre that her grandmother had stage-managed, she had to do something soon, before the old woman returned from her errand. Sitting helplessly on the bamboo platform, Aosenla seemed to emerge from naïve innocence to a rude awakening into knowledge: the knowledge that this marriage was going to be more than a simple match between a boy and a girl; it was going to be an alliance in which she was the most important figure, like the queen on a chessboard. What was happening on the platform seemed so unreal and so sudden, she felt like an actor on a stage who was being coerced to perform on cues from invisible prompters. Though she was an intelligent girl, she was too inexperienced and had failed to fully grasp the politics involved in the proposed alliance. And it was only now, stranded in this spot, that she realized how vulnerable she had been from the moment her father had received the proposal. And in the confined space of the platform, she felt like a cornered animal threatened with imminent capture or death at the hands of forces far superior to her own. It was an impossible position; the composure that she had managed to display through her open defiance at home had now been breached and self-doubt began to assail her.

But with a supreme effort, she reminded herself to stand firm and decided to utter a polite 'no' to the man sitting impassively before her. Just when she was about to speak, her cousin brought steaming cups of tea, she refused to have any, saying that she was not thirsty, but the girl left a cup by her side anyway. And then suddenly she reappeared and, coming straight to her, whispered in her ear, 'Father says not to scare him away.' But Aosenla had already resolved to say 'no' because her heart refused to say 'yes'. Yet, her mind was becoming increasingly scared about the consequences if she said 'no'. Meanwhile, Bendangmeren was showing signs of restlessness and was smoking continuously. Inside the house, her uncle was beginning to worry and had already sent for his mother to come and intervene. Just when Aosenla had mustered enough courage and was about to utter a definite 'no', the grandmother appeared on the platform. In a playful tone, she said to her granddaughter, 'Go inside, Asen, you have spent enough time with him, it is my turn to talk to him.' With a great sense of regret that she could not after all utter the definitive 'no', she left the platform and without acknowledging anyone in the kitchen, bolted from her uncle's house and rushed to her grandmother's. One of her cousins ran out after her, telling her to stop, but Aosenla had become deaf to her calls and entreaties. The old woman had observed her unceremonious departure but she stood resolutely near the flabbergasted man and began to talk fast. 'Please do not be offended by her words or behaviour. After all, what can you expect from an immature girl who has lived in town among alien people for so many years? It is not as if she is not willing to marry you; it is only the fancy ideas she has developed in school and college which are making her a little difficult. You will soon see she'll come around. As it is, both our families are in agreement, and especially her parents have assured us that she will listen to them. It is only the surprise and shock of seeing you so unexpectedly like this that has induced this reaction. You see, we did not tell her that you would be here. And besides, she did not say 'no' did she? So do not delay, see that the marriage takes place soon, next month if possible. Otherwise the marriage season will be over.' She then escorted the slightly puzzled man into the house for another round of tea and snacks.

Bendang, as he was popularly known, left the uncle's house in a thoughtful mood. His encounters with women were never like this; in fact he was immensely proud of his other conquests, and until very recently he was on very intimate terms with an older and experienced woman. It was precisely to stop him from marrying this other woman, that his father had started negotiations with Aosenla's relatives. The father did not approve of the other woman, not only because of her reputation, but more importantly because she came from a minor clan of the village. Having made good among the educated elite of his society, he wanted to consolidate the family's position through this alliance with a girl from a founding clan of the village. He was prepared to go to any lengths to see that his son married Aosenla and nobody else. The father at this moment however was not aware that his son had just come out of an encounter from which he did not emerge a clear winner. Contrary to the relatives' apprehensions about Aosenla's hostile attitude to the proposal, Bendang walked away from the meeting more resolute than ever to marry this girl. He actually felt challenged and was determined to have her precisely because she had displayed her reluctance to marry him so openly. No woman had so far been able to resist his charms and he was not going to be rejected by this slip of a girl. He was also encouraged by her own family's unabashed eagerness to see her married to him. As he walked back to his lodgings in the village, he remembered the grandmother's almost pleading statement about what transpired on the bamboo platform that night, 'She did not say no, did she?' implying that the fact was tantamount to saying 'yes'. Though his ego was hurt a little by the boldness of Aosenla's initial responses, Bendang was content in the knowledge that none of his friends would ever know exactly what had happened. He would simply go back to town boasting that he had won Aosenla's heart and that they were going to be married within the month.

The noose of matrimony was tightening around Aosenla's neck. But she was unaware of this and had returned to her grandmother's house in a somewhat triumphant mood; she thought that she had made it very clear to Bendang that she was not prepared to marry him and she could now go back home and pick up her studies again. So before her grandmother reached she closed the door to her room and went off to sleep in this euphoric state of mind. But she woke up in the wee hours of the morning with an odd sensation: this feeling of being 'liked' and 'wanted' was something new in her young life. She had never had a boy say such words to her, and coming from a man like Bendang, she felt 'elevated' to a new plane of understanding about the man-woman relationship. She also found the idea pleasing and wondered if she was in any way 'obliged', for courtesy's sake, not to reject the overture with an abrupt 'no'. So far as the rejection was concerned, she felt relieved that she did not get a chance to say an outright 'no' to the man on the bamboo platform the previous evening. She thought that after reaching home, she would persuade her parents to politely decline the offer of marriage on some pretext or the other, and her life would continue as before.

3

But in the meantime, unknown to her, a strange debate was in progress in her maternal uncle's house. The grandmother insisted that she wanted to tell her son-in-law in town to go ahead with the preparations immediately. But there seemed to be doubts in the minds of some of the others. And when one relative protested by saying that judging from Aosenla's behaviour, he could see that she was still unwilling to marry the boy, the old woman snapped at him, 'Keep quiet, she did not say "no", did she? Bendang told me that everything was fine between them.' The maternal uncle was also a bit hesitant to come to a hasty conclusion and said, 'Maybe we should ask the girl what actually happened tonight.' The old woman flared up and rejected that idea forthright, saying that it would be interpreted adversely by the boy's family and they might even call off the wedding. She challenged everyone in the room, 'Do you want this to happen? Do you want us to become the laughing stock of the village? Think of what will happen to the girl.' This was a real dampener and everyone became silent; deep in their hearts, they too wanted this alliance to be forged between their families. As the relatives were leaving the house, the elder who had spoken first looked at the uncle and said, 'If I were you, I would think over it once more,' and, without waiting for a reply, went off.

The grandmother was jolted out of her complacency by the note of dissent from the uncles and felt that unless she acted fast, her pet project might fall through. So she sent her own interpretation of Aosenla's meeting with Bendang to the girl's parents the very next morning, hinting that everything was settled between the two. The father immediately sent his emissary, in this case his nephew, formally accepting the offer of marriage, and immediately launched into frantic preparations for the wedding. When Aosenla reached home the next day, she was greeted by an unbelievable scene. Her father gave her a broad smile and her mother embraced her tearfully. It was a most unusual reception, especially from her father who always maintained his distance from her. To add to her confusion, the usually quiet household was abuzz with activities supervised by various aunts and cousins. The girl was bewildered and wanted to shout, 'What is going on?' But she realized that the activities were on account of her impending wedding, and she retired to her room without speaking to anyone. It became clear to her that her grandmother had somehow manipulated the outcome of her meeting with Bendang. Her mother later told her that based on the grandmother's message, her father had already sent the formal acceptance to the boy's family. She then knew that she was well and truly trapped. In spite of her own conviction that she had made her objection very clear to Bendang that night, she had begun to feel uneasy as soon as her grandmother pleaded with her to stay for one more day saying, 'Who knows, I may not last long and this may be our last visit.' She thought that the old woman was being melodramatic but now understood that she had planned the delay so that by the time Aosenla reached home, her father would have given the final commitment and her fate would have been sealed.

Perhaps it was during this short interlude before her

marriage, which seemed inevitable now, that Aosenla began to understand the pressure that a family, especially a traditional one like hers, can exert on an individual. The family had made it amply clear to her that their welfare and future hinged on this alliance. She still did not understand in what way, but when she saw the happiness on her parents' faces, she did not have the heart to protest any more. The defiance and resentment she had earlier felt was now being overtaken by a sense of resignation. Overwhelmed by the enormity of the collective pressure on her, she simply withdrew into a shell and an acute sense of her aloneness subdued her otherwise vibrant personality. Bewildered, helpless, caught in the inevitability of the wedding and swamped in the whirlwind preparations, she dared not voice any more protests. In utter dejection, she withdrew into herself and became a passive spectator, maintaining a stoic silence whenever the subject of her marriage was brought up. This silence was interpreted as the natural shyness of a bride-to-be. After receiving the final word of acceptance, Bendang's father lost no time at all in mounting their own preparations in great style for what was being touted as the grandest wedding in the town. In traditional weddings, the onus of feeding wedding guests and bearing all other expenses was on the groom's family. So busloads of relatives were transported from the village a week ahead of the big event, housed and treated to sumptuous feasts every day. The small town was agog with reports of how many kinds of animals were being slaughtered every day for these feasts. Family and friends from neighbouring villages were brought daily to the town to join the pre-wedding celebrations.

In the excitement and fanfare of the preparations, only one person seemed left out: the bride-to-be. She was not consulted about the date; she heard of it for the first time from a cousin. Her measurements were taken for the gown, but it was Bendang's sisters who chose the material and the design. But on one point she put her foot down; she wanted a particular cousin to be her bridesmaid, and in spite of protests that the cousin was older than her, she had her way. So on the appointed day, the reluctant bride wore the white garments of her transition to another life: gown, veil and gloves and matching high-heeled shoes that she would wear for the first time in her life. A day earlier, when the shoes were brought to her for fitting, she had stared at them for some time and burst into uncontrollable giggles. The women around her began to exchange knowing looks; already there were whispers among the womenfolk that Aosenla was behaving strangely, and seemed to be avoiding even friends and relatives, which some said was due to her pride at having caught the fancy of one of the town's most eligible bachelors. The women of course did not know why she was reacting in this manner and continued to look at her with suspicion; what they could not know was that Aosenla was reminded of the first pair of grown-up shoes that she'd worn as a young girl. They were hand-me-downs from an aunt who had gotten tired of wearing them. How she treasured those battered shoes! She wore them to church and at other formal occasions even though they were a size too big for her. She knew that other girls sniggered behind her back but she did not care; all that mattered to her was that the adult shoes belonged to her. And now when she suddenly became aware of the strange silence around her, she pulled herself together and tried on the wedding shoes. They pinched a bit but she simply nodded to indicate that they were all right.

4

The memory of the shoes pinching brought her back to the present. She bent down to massage her right foot absent-mindedly and in the process the wedding invitation slipped from her hand. As she became aware of where she was and what she was doing, she asked herself what had brought on these disturbing thoughts in the first place. She got up to go inside, and as she did so, her foot trod on the fallen card, but she ignored it and groped her way to the bedroom where there was light. She began pacing in the room, trying to remember what she was supposed to be doing this evening, when she heard Bendang's jeep turn into the compound. It was not so long ago, she thought wryly, that she used to strain to listen to the sound of a vehicle entering their compound and determine if it was his. She claimed that she could recognize the distinctive roar of the engine and say accurately that it was Bendang's 4x4 Willy's jeep. But now, even when he entered the bedroom, she remained rooted to the spot where she stood, indifferent to his presence.

When he saw her still in her casual dress, he asked in a complaining voice, 'Why are you not dressed for the party?'

She replied vaguely, 'What party?'

'Why, don't you remember I told you that we have been invited to the Brigadier's party tonight?'

'You go, I am not feeling well.'

At her reply, he became angry and began to shout at her, 'Are you trying to let me down again? You refused to come to the Deputy Commissioner's party last week, and do you know what everyone was saying? That you have become too good for me with your glib talk about world affairs, books and music. Actually, you know nothing about life except your pretensions based on book knowledge. Hah! Who cares for your phony accomplishments; you are still my wife, and you will have to come tonight because I promised my friend the Brigade Major that you would be there.'

At this impassioned speech, she looked at him with a new understanding; lately he had begun to tell her how his friends' wives were playing important roles in getting favours for their husbands like lucrative portfolios, and even coveted postings to business districts. He mentioned the name of one of his friends who, he claimed, beat him to a fat contract because of the 'influence' of the other's wife over the Chief Engineer. It was the tone in which he had earlier mentioned his promise to the army officer that made her recoil as though at an unnameable danger, and she began to curse herself for her naiveté in once thinking that there could be true love and mutual understanding between them. But she brushed aside that stinging regret and, without saying anything, meekly changed into an evening outfit to accompany him to the party. When he saw her, he was visibly pleased, and even tried to make conversation during the drive through town. She responded in monosyllables. Expectant of getting free drinks and mingling with the town's so-called elite, Bendang good-humoredly ignored her sulk. Once they arrived at the venue, he made a beeline for the bar, leaving her to fend for herself. Aosenla, by now, had become quite adept at holding her own in parties such as these. Gone were the awkward ways and uninhibited talk that had marked the early years of her married life.

As she stood making small talk with the Assam Rifles' Commandant's wife, holding a glass of rum and Coca-Cola in her hand, she could not help remembering her first party where she had made a spectacle of herself by first spilling someone's whisky as she tottered on high heels, and then dropping her fork with a clatter as she tried to grapple with a stubborn piece of chicken! But she had long overcome her social gaucherie, and had become quite adept at gliding through crowds with ease. Tonight too, with sips of the soothing drink, her earlier despondent mood slowly dissipated and she began to enjoy being in the midst of all these well-dressed men and women. But she was not yet ready to indulge in sweet nothings with the animated ladies who were already quite 'happy'. So she gradually drifted to a corner of the big hall and sat down by herself. The soft music began to revive her spirits. It was an instrumental number played in the rhythm of a slow foxtrot. Engrossed in the melody and rhythm of the music, she began to tap her feet and before she realized it, the Brigade Major was asking her for a dance. She was confused; Bendang was nowhere to be seen and there were no other couples on the floor. She began to protest, saying that she was sitting down because she was feeling a little out of sorts. The officer was too well-bred to make a fuss and he withdrew. The rest of the evening went off uneventfully, and after an unremarkable meal, they reached home by midnight.

Once inside the house, Aosenla was accosted by an irate Bendang who started to berate her. He accused her of being impolite in civilized society, and when she countered by asking how, he cited her refusal to dance with the host. He added that the Major was fuming at this 'public' humiliation and this affront might cost Bendang his precious goodwill, which he had so assiduously cultivated the last few months. Aosenla saw that her husband was quite drunk and his words slurred out of his mouth like sludge.

He continued, 'Do you know what he said? He said that my wife is snooty, thinks no end of herself and does not know how to behave in polite society. Mind you, if I do not get the army contract this year, it will be your fault.'

Aosenla was shocked; instead of feeling the guilt that her husband was trying to burden her with, a strange emotion was overtaking her. She felt soiled by the insinuation in his words. What kind of a man was he becoming that he thought nothing of using his own wife as bait for some army contracts? It was as though the image of this man she had so carefully built was diminishing in front of her eyes. Strangely though, instead of getting angry, she began to look at him with immense pity and was gripped by the realization that something vital in their relationship had snapped. She saw that there was no point in arguing with a man so insensitive and already so befuddled by liquor and anger. So, to restore a semblance of peace, she quietly mumbled 'sorry' and proceeded to prepare herself for bed. Bendang too was beginning to feel the effect of the alcohol in his system and though physically he felt tired, he had retained enough sobriety to realize the implication of his angry outburst. He seemed to lose all his anger at once and mechanically kicked off his shoes and socks, somehow got rid of his shirt and pants and was soon sleeping the sleep of the dead drunk. Aosenla, however, was not able to go to sleep; her mind was in turmoil. The enormity of the insinuation in her husband's words so rattled her that she began to tremble uncontrollably.

As she lay in the far corner of the big bed, she thought back to her marriage again. The event itself was memorable for the garish ostentation of the noveaux riche where she was the essential centrepiece. Once it was evident that there was no way out of it, she had resigned herself to it and had begun to concentrate on the man who had become not only her husband but everything else besides. In the heady aftermath of the event, with the numerous wedding presents, new clothes and a brand-new house where she was the sole mistress, she went into a mood of euphoria and started to weave a fiction of love for him: planning how she would become the ideal wife to earn his love and respect, and how she would 'reform' him from his drinking and gambling and build an ideal marriage. In fact her relatives, and especially her mother-in-law, had repeatedly reminded her of this responsibility. They told her, 'Remember, it is the wife who has to guide and help the man to become a good husband,' and went on to enumerate the various cases where the wives had performed miracles in restoring drunks to temperance and had transformed wife-bashers to devout church-goers. It was a tall order for a teenage bride but she took their words to heart and added her own romantic notions of married life. This, in spite of the fact that this man had on many occasions openly boasted to her of his many conquests. She tried to console herself by saying that what happened before her marriage was water under the bridge and that her mission in life now was to win him over with love and understanding.

Her idealistic notions about love and life were further fuelled by her reading of romantic novels where the heroine always emerged triumphant, and the rake, reformed. Just like the heroines of the novels, she developed the notion that she was indeed in love with her husband and that her devotion alone would eventually succeed in bringing this egotistical man into the circle of her love. Years later, she was to admit that what she had failed to recognize in the early days of her marriage was the fact that she was married to a man who was clearly incapable of reciprocating any of the feelings she had so carefully nurtured. She was too inexperienced and too idealistic to make any impression on a man already set in his ways. His vision of life was too narrow; all that he cared about was to make as much money as possible, own the best car, drink the best whiskey and to have a docile wife who would always do his bidding. For him, the sole purpose of the wife was to enhance his image in society. Aosenla, however, wove fantasies about creating a new space where love would flourish and she would cherish him in that 'circle of love'. She had hoped that he would also cherish her, and their new life would be perfect. But ironically, the man whom she had set out to reform and install almost as a god in her dream-world would eventually change her vision of life forever.

5

As part of her efforts to create shared interests, Aosenla had tried to encourage her husband to cultivate the habit of reading books. But Bendang was dismissive of books: he said, 'Books give people wrong ideas.' And every time she ordered books by post, he would make a scene, claiming that she was spending too much money on 'unnecessary' things. She liked to listen to the radio: BBC, VOA, and Radio Ceylon not only for news but also for the different programmes and the beautiful music they broadcast. She also read all kinds of magazines and newspapers: in short, any word that was printed. These were pastimes that he often said were not appropriate for a married woman. Though Aosenla derived great pleasure and comfort from these activities, they soon became another source of conflict between them, and her husband began staying away from home more and more.

The first time that she waited up for him to come home for dinner, she had fallen asleep on the dining table and woke only when there was a loud banging on the door. When the man saw that she had waited up for him, he burst out laughing and began to mock her: 'Hey, why are you behaving like a wife from the plains? Did I ask you to wait up for me? How silly you are.' It was apparent that he had eaten somewhere and did not care whether his wife ate or not.

Looking back on the innumerable instances when her husband belittled her or ignored her for long periods of time, Aosenla began to wonder why she had clung to her dream of finding real happiness or love with this man. It was as though she had been ensnared by her own web of unrealistic expectations. That night, when she finally fell asleep, she dreamt that she was tumbling into a dark unending tunnel where flashes of lightning illuminated horrible nightmarish images of creatures that were trying to tear her to pieces.

Her love of books and discussions about them and the authors brought her into close contact with her youngest brother-in-law Sentinungsang's circle of friends whenever he came home for the holidays from his college in Allahabad. Many of his friends would come to the house to play badminton or simply chat about books and music over endless cups of tea. They would then invariably troop into Aosenla's house to listen to more music or ask her what she was currently reading. Aosenla had somehow wheedled a record-player from Bendang one day when he was in a good mood, and soon acquired a collection of her own which included mostly instrumental music by groups like Billy Vaughn and his Orchestra, The Shadows, The Ventures, Mantovani, Ray Anthony, and of course all the songs of the Beatles. Their music may not have been classic but the tunes and orchestrations were soothing to the ears, and many were adaptations of popular songs, and she could hum along with them in imagined harmony. She enjoyed the company of these young men with whom she could freely exchange views about their various interests. They also belonged to her own age group, which made her feel at ease with them.

One boy among them particularly fascinated her. His name was Merentoshi, Toshi for short. He was a talented singer and could sing just like Cliff Richard, who was at the top of the charts in those days. He was also fond of reading books, but not the 'silly' ones that she confessed to reading. It was through him that she was introduced to a more varied bunch of writers like Somerset Maugham, Pearl Buck, Hemingway, Boris Pasternak, Tolstoy, Dostoyevsky, Gorky, and others. In the small-town environment of Mokokchung in the sixties, these authors opened a completely different world for Aosenla and she believed that a new dimension was being added to her limited existence. When this group met in her house, she felt animated and different; she felt more 'alive'. Even Bendang noticed the change in her the few times he happened to come home while they were there, and he began to accuse her of flirting with the young men. He even scolded his brother for bringing them to the house and 'encouraging' her in such behaviour that was so unbecoming for a married woman.

Things came to a head that summer when she agreed to help her cousin Imlirenla. She was a teacher in a kindergarten school, and had asked Aosenla to help her prepare an item for a variety show the school was organizing before the summer vacation. Her class was to present a song for which Aren chose the song *Doe a Deer* from the movie *Sound of Music.* Since Aosenla had the sound track of the movie, she wrote down the words and made the children memorize them. But trouble began when they tried to teach them the tune. Neither of them was good at singing and did not know how to make the children sing in harmony or with proper timing. It was then that Aren came up with the idea of enlisting Toshi's help, as everyone knew how good a singer he was. He readily agreed to help them. So for about a week, Aosenla went to the town hall where the concert was going to be staged and the three of them would make the children sing. Realizing that without a musical back-up the children's voices would not sound good, Toshi invited some of his friends to bring their instruments and help out the two inept choir-masters. They trooped in with guitars, a set of drums and even a pair of cymbals. The effect was magical. The children were completely mesmerized by these musicians and even the shyest ones began to sing at the top of their voices. The song was promising to be the star item of the whole show. Aren and Aosenla were elated. On the final day of rehearsal, they ordered tea and snacks from a nearby canteen and the boys started to sing and entertain the children. Aosenla went home that evening in a jubilant mood; she had been able, she thought, to contribute a little to the success of the concert, and she also admitted to herself that she enjoyed these sessions especially because she could be in the company of Toshi. What she did not know was that her outings were being monitored and reported to Bendang by a busybody, a notorious gossip who also happened to be a distant cousin of his mother. Her house was located near the hall, and in the story she told, Aosenla was seen with Toshi all the time laughing and joking freely. The aunt said the song practice was only an excuse; Aosenla was going there to meet this boy who, she said, was a notorious womanizer and that Bendang had better look out or his young wife would fall for this charming Romeo.

When Aosenla reached home the evening before the concert day, it was dusk and at first she could not make out the people who were waiting for her in the living room. She stepped in and said light-heartedly, 'Hey why are you all sitting in the dark?' and proceeded to switch on the lights, but then stopped in her tracks: Bendang's sisters and his mother and his maternal uncle were sitting glum-faced and stern. She did not know what to say. Her mother-in-law ordered her to sit, and then Bendang started with the accusations, 'Where have you been all this while?'

Aosenla answered, 'You know perfectly well where I have been. I asked you if I could help out Aren and you said it was all right.'

'But that is only an excuse, right?', the sister-in-law shouted. 'You go there to meet your boyfriend, don't you?'

'What boyfriend?'

'Don't act innocent; we know everything about you and that no-good womanizer,' Bendang growled.

The mother-in-law then launched into a tirade about wayward daughters-in-law and how their sins would be visited upon the children.

'A mother's place is in the house and instead of being there to attend to their needs, you go gallivanting around town and come home so late. Aren't you ashamed of your behaviour?'

The scene unfolding before her was unreal and Aosenla felt like screaming at the top of her voice. Instead, she calmly said, 'Tonight was the last rehearsal, and if you want to know the truth go and ask Aren; I was with her all these days.'

'You mean to say that Toshi was not there?'

'Of course he was there, so were four of his friends, the other teachers of the school, and about a hundred children,' Aosenla answered defiantly.

At this, Bendang jumped up angrily and was about to slap her but his uncle restrained him and he sat down muttering, 'I am going to kill that bastard.' His other sister turned to him and said mockingly, 'Why don't you take care of your own wife first before going after that man? What if he turns around and says, "What can I do? Your wife came running after me!" Where will you be then?'

Aosenla could no longer tolerate these accusations and stood up angrily because unlike the crestfallen adulteress brought before Jesus by the Pharisees and Sadducees, she did not require a saviour in this bizarre family court as she had not committed a 'sin'. This truth gave her the courage to say what she did next and if the people in that room had expected her to cower before the strength of their numbers, they were in for a big surprise. She felt a greater outrage towards Bendang, who seemed to have abandoned her to the public invasion into their marriage through this attempt to 'shame' her. Though she was terribly shaken and almost in tears, Aosenla steeled herself and measuring her words carefully, threw this challenge at them, 'I do not know from where you got this absurd idea about a boyfriend. This is a grave accusation and I am not prepared to let this unfounded attack on my integrity go unchallenged. After all I too have a family and clan members; I have not sprung out of sticks or stones. I shall send word to my father, uncles and other clan members and only in their presence can we have a proper hearing to determine if there is any truth in your accusation; it is not going to be settled like this with all of you ganging up on me. And not only that, you will have to deal with Toshi's family too because you are naming him as my "boyfriend". Be prepared for that too.'

With these words she walked out of the room in a huff, leaving Bendang and his relatives in stunned silence. They had never expected Aosenla to stand up to them in this manner, especially Bendang who had taken her so much for granted that he always thought of her as someone who had nobody in the world except himself. They continued to sit in silence for some more time and it was the maternal uncle who finally spoke. From his tone, it was apparent that he had all along been a reluctant participant in the family farce.

'Didn't I warn you to make sure of all the facts before accusing her in this manner? How can you believe that woman's words? Don't you know how many marriages she has tried to harm by her evil tongue? If it comes to a hearing of the families, I must warn you sister, I shall not attend it because you people have no evidence against her, just the malicious gossip of a scandal-monger.'

He walked out in a huff, leaving behind a shocked silence.

The daughter-in-law, whom they had always considered to be in awe of their supposedly superior position, had stumped them not only with a moral challenge, but had also reminded them that she had the advantage of belonging to a powerful clan in the village. She had succeeded in warning them that they could not level such serious charges against merely on hearsay. They left the house not only chastised but also feeling small before this girl who seemed to have gained a new stature in a most unexpected way. As for Bendang, his escape was in liquor, and that night he drank so much that he fell asleep on the sofa in the living room without having any dinner. Aosenla simply bolted the door of their bedroom and went off to sleep, feeling calm and detached from everything and everyone around her, especially Bendang.

When the father-in-law discovered what had happened, he berated his wife and daughters with harsh words and sent for Bendang for a private conversation. No one knew what was said but there seemed to be a definite change in the son's behaviour following this incident.

Afterwards, when she mulled over the events of the evening, Aosenla wondered where she had got the courage from to speak like that and invoke the involvement of her family and other clan members so spontaneously. And bringing in Toshi's family was also an unexpectedly clever stroke. But her desperate ploy seemed to have worked; the subdued behaviour of the people in the big house was evidence of this. Perhaps that night, by asserting her right to protect herself, Aosenla did indeed come into her own, stepping across another threshold where she claimed her rightful place in a family that had treated her as someone of little consequence. The incident wrong-footed Bendang's family, who did not know exactly how to deal with her now. They still held on to their bias against her but now could not openly say things to discredit her anymore. There was a studied silence instead of the constant barbed remarks about her ineptitude. Bendang was in the habit of always extolling the virtues of his sisters who studied in a smart college in Delhi. On such occasions, Aosenla used to feel like a dirty rag in comparison to their various accomplishments: the way they dressed in western clothes, had their hair cut short, and wore heavy make-up even at home. They knew the latest dances and often spoke of going out on dates with foreign students to the city's hottest nightspots. Talking about his sisters' social graces and accomplishments was her husband's way of reminding his wife that she had come into this marriage with a handicap: she would never be on an equal footing with his family's status and wealth. This realization would invariably send her into prolonged periods of depression and self-doubt. But that night Aosenla felt that she had taken an important step towards asserting herself and demanding due respect as an equal among them.

After the incident, which had backfired on the family so badly, Aosenla re-assessed her situation and decided that she had to be more assertive and take hold of her life. She began introspecting and came to the conclusion that she ought to try and establish herself on level terms with the rest of his family, especially his sisters. In order to do that, she began to take more care over her personal grooming and acquired a new and more fashionable wardrobe. Within a short time, they noticed that she was using lipstick and light make-up when she went to church. Though she had given birth to two children, Aosenla had maintained her youthful figure and the modern outfits enhanced this to her advantage. The remarkable transformation brought about by meticulous personal grooming and up-to-date clothes caught everyone's attention: people in party circles especially noticed this change and began talking about her as a late-blooming beauty. She noticed their admiring glances and this pleased her immensely because she was out to make a point to Bendang and her snobbish in-laws and she knew she was succeeding. She also understood that her constant efforts at 'educating' herself through reading and listening to music had been not only to satisfy her natural appetite for these but perhaps also an unconscious way of shoring up her fragile self-esteem. By assuming this new persona, she began to believe in herself a little more, and if the current project was a 'flaunting' of her visible attributes, so be it, she told herself, and admitted that she was revelling in it! She took meticulous care to nurture her public persona almost like a weapon of self-defense against a family that laid so much stress on appearances. She remembered how pleased she had been when she had managed to score a point over her rich classmates by managing to hold on to the first position in class every year. Though they were superior to her in material things, her achievement in her studies was something which neither their wealth nor family status could ever buy. Acutely aware of her poverty and the humble circumstances of her family, this fact gave her great comfort, and sustained her ego throughout her school years. In her present 'triumph' too, she was experiencing the same heady exultation, but in a strange way, it also had a mellowing effect on her recent mood of defiance and antagonism towards her husband and his family, lulling her into a state of complacent magnanimity. What she failed to recognize then was the fact that in the limited environs of her school, the annual first prize was sufficient for the day. But this was an adult life where one has to deal with the extremely volatile intricacies of human relationships constantly and where 'scoring' highly was never enough.

The public acknowledgement and admiration of Aosenla's 'coming of age' as it were, created a different sort of impact on Bendang. In a curious contrast to his belligerence of the 'confrontation' night, Bendang's attitude seemed to have undergone a sea change. He had become more attentive to her and stayed away from his gambling and drinking parties. His business trips too were curtailed to a minimum. Aosenla was quite taken in by these changes in her husband's behaviour. She did not realize that his efforts were not so much in appreciation of her integrity or her new persona but more so to circumvent her indignation at being accused unjustly, so that her threat of calling for a clan meeting would be forgotten. Aosenla, in the meantime, was enjoying her newfound persona and the solicitous attention of her husband and she was truly happy. She began to think that now the proposed meeting that she had threatened them with, would serve no purpose; although she knew she would be vindicated in any such meeting, but the whole town would come to know that her character had become the subject of speculation. She was intelligent enough to realize that some traces of suspicion would always remain in the minds of people about her. Because of this instinctive caution for self-preservation, she did not pursue the matter any further and instead immersed herself in numerous social activities: going out to parties often and participating in all public events.

At home too the mood was one of celebration. Through his subterfuge, Bendang was able to create an atmosphere of harmonious domesticity, a feeling she had not enjoyed before. Deluding herself that she was succeeding in her efforts to gain his love and attention and being gullible and vulnerable in her inherent romanticism, she once more lapsed into the role of dutiful wife and mother. She began to think that she was at last winning the battle of 'reforming' her husband and readily forgave him the many insults and indignities he had inflicted on her. He displayed more ardour in his lovemaking and this seemed to release a dormant spring of physicality in her. Whereas before the conjugal act was a perfunctory ritual, she was beginning to actually enjoy it now, which she thought was part of the 'triumph' of her new self. Her own physical fulfilment only heightened her sense of imagined success in bringing this man into the circle of her love. And within two months of such idyllic happiness, she realized that she was pregnant again. Then the inevitable happened. As soon as the doctor confirmed it, contrary to all her romantic expectations, her husband began to drift back to his former self. It was then that reality took over and Aosenla was once more left alone to nurse her bruised ego, feeling used and discarded. What hurt and frightened her most now was the recognition that she had fallen prey to her own ideas about her imagined self, and discovered how fragile that self was. She also realized with a shock that it was her newly awakened sexuality that had enlarged her vulnerability.

6

In the months that followed, as she tried to take stock of the turnaround in their relationship, Aosenla began to question her own role in this interlude and in the deep recesses of her mind she began to feel 'condemned' by her own uninhibited sexuality, which she had 'used' in a desperate attempt to keep him under her spell. She also became aware that not only she but Bendang too had fallen back on this age-old strategy in the contest between them: he, to re-affirm his superiority over her body once more, and she, to create a niche in his mind for herself. So what was the difference between them? This thought had a sickening effect on her, even as she tried to justify her own actions by saying that what she did was out of genuine love while his seeming ardour had been just a cheap and detestable ploy. But in spite of all such attempts at self-justification, there remained at the back of her mind the growing awareness that she was walking a tightrope on the thin line separating 'sex-as-love' and 'sex-as-means', and the more she thought about this, the more frightened she became about this inherent dichotomy of love and sex between man and woman. In this deep mood of introspection, Aosenla had to admit that her own sexuality was an intimidating discovery and that she had indeed 'used' it as a means towards some kind of pacification-reconciliation or even as retrieval of the missing ingredient in her marriage.

But now, the aftermath of this charade between husband and wife left her bruised and burdened with the knowledge of her vulnerability. For Bendang, once he had achieved the submission of his wife through the brief interlude of physical closeness, life became 'normal' for him. The old drinking and gambling parties were revived, business trips became inevitably longer, and the husband and wife retreated to their separate worlds once more. Throughout, one regret remained: if only, he had given her even a little hint of love, she thought, the entire business about sex and love would not have assumed such sinister proportions.

While mulling over these thoughts one afternoon, Aosenla suddenly remembered an 'encounter' she had had with an older man during her childhood. It was a period when her parents were away, and she and her brothers were being chaperoned by an old aunt. She and her younger brother would come home from school mid-morning and for all practical purposes would be on their own, because their old aunt liked to spend most of her time lolling on the bed or pottering around in the kitchen. Left to their own devices, the youngsters had to find ways to keep themselves occupied and one of those was to visit a shack near their house, where temporary labourers from their village used to stay. Having nothing else to do, the young girl and her brother used to go to this camp quite often and watch people cook or wash their clothes. The labourers hardly took any notice of them. But one of the men befriended them and soon began buying them sweets and biscuits. One day Aosenla went there alone and the man called her aside and said to her, 'If you do what I ask you to do, I'll buy you anything you want.' She was hesitant at first and did not reply. When he repeated his offer, she remembered that she had secretly wanted a pair of dangling earrings she had seen in the Marwari shop on the road to school and was planning to ask her father to buy them for her. But the truth was that it would be to her mother that she would have to go with this request because she was in great awe of her father, who did not say much and was always talking of how poor they were. She also knew that her timid mother would never muster enough courage to convey the daughter's wish to her husband. Though young, Aosenla somehow sensed that her mother was in perpetual dread of her father. So the prospect of getting the earrings through her mother's intercession seemed remote. She had therefore reluctantly given up the idea, but now this man was telling her that he would give her anything if she did what he wanted. She could not resist the temptation and told the man that she would tell him the next day. Though she was young, she was clever enough to make sure that the earrings were still in the shop before she agreed to his condition. She ran all the way to the shop and peeped inside. Ah, they were still there! She ran back to the camp to tell the man but he had gone back to work after his mid-day meal.

The next morning before she went to school she sneaked out to the camp and caught the man on his way to work and told him what she wanted. He said he would buy the earrings on his way back and told her to come by during the lunch break. That day Aosenla ran all the way from school, telling her brother that she had an upset stomach and before he reached home, she ran on to the camp. She found the man waiting. She wanted to see the earrings, but the man said, 'You have to do what I want first.' But the young girl insisted that he show her what he had in his hand. The man held the dangling earrings away from her reach, and said, 'Come inside now,' and closed the door. She watched in innocent fascination as he pulled down his pants and squatted on a low stool. He spread out his thighs and pulled her closer and took off her panties. He was breathing hard and told her to sit on his organ, which was now standing erect like a pestle. The little girl did not understand what he was asking her to do, and asked, 'Why?' He merely pulled her closer and tried to pull her on to his extended thing telling her to spread herself wider. But nothing happened except that she began to feel a bit of pain and tried to squirm away from that impossible position. He was sweating now and had a strange look on his face but even after several attempts he could not push his thing into her. He was getting impatient and also worried because it was taking more time than he expected. Aosenla was by now scared. When, distracted by a sound from outside, the man's grip on her loosened, she suddenly slipped out of his grasp, and picking up her panties hurriedly put them on even as the man was scrambling to his feet from the awkward position of squatting almost on the floor. He tried to grab her but she had already run out of the house leaving the naked man inside the house shouting, 'Hey come back, don't you want these?' She was truly frightened now and without a backward glance ran on. From a distance she saw her brother going towards the house and when they met up, they went home hand-in-hand. She never visited the camp again and as all transient workers do, the man also disappeared one day. It was only after many years that the full implications of what might have happened became clear to her and she would shudder in secret at the recollection of the hideous scenario. Aosenla had subconsciously tried to erase this episode from her mind, even pretending that it never happened and that it was only a bad dream.

But in the secret recesses of her mind she had always felt sullied and dirtied and her recent sexual encounters with her husband seemed to reinforce this sense of self-loathing with such a force that she wanted to undo whatever had happened to her body as a result of this. The nightmare of this childhood experience was now totally reversed; she was the one who had dangled her sex in a desperate bid to 'earn' her husband's love. She had become the temptress, the enticer, the manipulator and the shameless seductress. Often, she wished she were devoid of any sexual impulses, that she could get rid of the 'female-ness' in her body. The sudden drop from the heights of both physical satisfaction and imagined emotional fulfilment was such that at times she wanted to obliterate her 'self' and become something without a form. She also wished that her brain and mind would stop functioning. But a small voice within her mounted a relentless campaign, urging her to fight the futile fuming and pick up pieces of her life and make some sense of her recent behaviour.

It was not easy, this effort to tame her wild thoughts. It drained her both physically and mentally. Her mind constantly went back to the encounter with the older man, but the fear she had felt then was nothing like the sense of self-abasement that assaulted her now. The little girl of the past did not know what the man wanted; she did not even know that such a thing as sex existed! She had only coveted a piece of shining costume jewellery. But Aosenla, the married woman, had consciously entered into an unspoken bargain of bodies. The husband too, as his subsequent behaviour proved, had only used his conjugal rights to establish his domination over her by impregnating her. She had to admit that just as much as her husband, she too was a willing participant in this sordid barter and for her, at the end of the idyllic interlude of romantic sex as she had believed it to be, she was left bruised and battered emotionally and had to cope with the physical certainty of yet another pregnancy. If at first she was overwhelmed by a great sense of betrayal and abandonment by her husband, to her great mortification, she had to admit that she could not claim to have lost his love and respect because she had never had them in the first place. For him, she was simply a malleable agent in his scheme of things who also happened to be his wife. And he had exercised his rights as a husband to 'tame' her. Once she realized this, the illusion of winning his heart was shattered forever.

The disillusionment about her expectations from her husband, however, paled before her own sense of self-indictment and recrimination. She went to the extent of asking herself if she was in any way different from all those women who peddle their bodies in the open market for hard cash. They counted their returns in rupees and for her, a respectably married woman, what was the currency she had expected from her husband? In the mis-directed attempt at gaining his love, she had proffered sex and was as guilty as he of using sex as means to a desired goal. He initiated the process of course, because he once again wanted to subdue her, and she succumbed to it because of a naïve sense of romantic idealism that she had concocted about their relationship. She had used her body as legitimate tender in order to secure his affection, if not outright love. But unfortunately, she had not foreseen what would happen if her plan failed. The one weapon at her disposal was once and for all neutralized because ultimately it was he who had established his superiority over her. He came out victorious from this skirmish, but for Aosenla, this 'disaster' only proved how vulnerable she was both psychologically and physically.

After weeks of 'mourning' for her naiveté and even stupidity, Aosenla began to take stock of her present situation. The 'disaster', as she thought of it earlier, was more in reference to her relationship with her husband than to her being pregnant again. She reminded herself that she could not and would not think of the child growing in her as a 'disaster' no matter what the circumstances of its conception. Once again she had to brace herself to cope with the situation because she realized that her survival not only as a wife but also a woman was at stake. So she began to take more interest not only in her daughters but also in the general management of the house and grounds. Now that it was known in the close family circle that she was pregnant again, she knew that there would be direct and indirect hints about their expectations that the child should be a boy. She remembered the long faces around the birthing bed both times when the midwife had disclosed that she had given birth to girls. Even she echoed the disappointment of the family when the second daughter was born. 'What is it?' the mother-in-law had demanded and the midwife had muttered, 'Not what you wanted.' She began to wonder what would happen if she gave birth to another daughter. Would her husband use the fact to look for another wife? It was known in rural societies that a wife could be turned out of the house if she proved to be barren. But she had not heard of any incidents where the husband could use the birth of daughters as a legitimate cause for divorce. This fact however did not give her any consolation and she too began to wish for a son to please her husband and keep her in-laws happy. Also, the present circumstance was totally different from the two earlier pregnancies; the prospect of motherhood earlier was welcomed with hope and excitement because of the apparently 'normal' process of conception. But this time around, she had to admit, her feelings were somewhat clouded over by her conviction of the 'false' pretense under which the child had been conceived.

As things turned out, the third pregnancy turned out to be a difficult one; there was one complication after another. In the third month, she became so anaemic that she had to be given several courses of injections to increase her haemoglobin count. Then she developed a severe chest infection for which she had to be hospitalized for two weeks. And in the eighth month during a routine check-up, it was discovered that the baby had shifted to a horizontal position that was blocking the birthing passage. She had to have daily manipulative massages to bring the baby slowly to the normal position. The progress was slow and at the end of the month, the doctor prescribed complete bed rest and advised hospitalization so that the massages could continue more regularly and the doctor could keep a close watch over her. On the home front too, things were not good; the moment Aosenla was admitted in the hospital, Bendang announced that he had to go to another town on business, and if the expectant mother felt let down by her husband, she did her best not to show it. Only her faithful maid sensed it and consoled her mistress by saying, 'Do not worry madam, I have told my brother to come and help us out if necessary.'

7

Five anxious days after the due date, the pains started and continued for six long hours without any of the normal indications of an imminent birth. From the worried looks on the faces of the doctors and nurses, Aosenla knew that there was something terribly wrong with this delivery. After consultations with his colleagues, her doctor decided to do a caesarean section in order to save both the child and the mother, and as Bendang was not available, he asked and received the consent from Aosenla herself. The operation was complicated, took more than three hours and when she awoke in the recovery room, there was only her maid and a yawning nurse. She asked for her husband but the maid simply shook her head. 'What about mummy?' meaning her mother-in-law. The maid replied, 'She came for a short while but she left screaming after the doctor told her something.' Aosenla seemed exhausted by the effort of speaking and remained quiet for a while. Finally, with a terrible sense of foreboding, she enquired feebly, 'Where is the baby?' At this, the maid averted her eyes and started to sniff. The old nurse pushed the maid out of the room and made soothing sounds and said, 'Shh, go back to sleep, you are still very weak; I'll bring the baby to you later.' But Aosenla refused to listen to her and wailed, 'No, where is my baby, I want my baby now.' The nurse tried to calm her down once again but even though exhausted, the young mother only became more agitated. So the nurse rang the bell and when a frightened student nurse appeared, told her to stay with the patient and ran to report to her superiors. She soon came back with a syringe, which she pushed into Aosenla, and began to swab her sweating brow with a wet towel. The medicine took immediate effect and Aosenla once more slumped into a sedated sleep.

When she finally awoke early the next morning, she found that she had been moved into a private cabin with bright pink curtains and saw a vase of flowers on the side table. She recognized the flowers to be from her own garden, the golden yellow roses which she had ordered from Bangalore and had tended so lovingly. For a few fleeting moments she was delighted to see the tender loving care she had lavished on the plants now yielding such beauty. But immediately she realized with a shock that she had not yet had a glimpse of her baby. She yanked at the bell-cord and a young nurse came in, almost running. 'Where is my baby?' demanded Aosenla, and the young girl stopped in her tracks. Again she shouted, 'Where is my baby? Bring her to me.' Only after she said 'her' Aosenla realized that she had actually said it and it dawned on her that she had all the time thought that since this baby was also a girl, her husband, mother-in-law and even the nurses were reluctant to show her the baby. Or, she suspected that it had been born with some deformity. The nurse looked on miserably and after some time left the room quietly. Left alone now, Aosenla became aware for the first time, of a strangeness about her body; her stomach was flat once again, which was to be expected. But there were bandages wrapped around it and she was beginning to feel the onslaught of a terrible pain. She tried to sit up and scream but no sound came; it was as if her vocal cords were clamped shut by the excruciating pain. Soon a peculiar tiredness overwhelmed her and she slumped back on her pillow and gave in to a welcome oblivion.

The second awakening, induced by cold sprinkles and gentle slapping of the cheeks, was fraught with such pain that she wanted to go under once more. But the tubes and pipes attached to her body were reviving her and she had to endure the pains of coming back to life. They added some painkillers to the tube and towards evening the pains became dull aches and she could swallow some watery soup. Still no baby, and when she asked about her husband, she was told that he had come the previous night when she was sleeping and had stayed only for a few minutes. She thought with disappointment and resignation, so be it; it was not her fault that this child too was a girl. But boy or girl, it was precious for her; besides, she was beginning to lactate and longed to put the baby to her swelling breasts. She pulled on the bell-cord once again and a different nurse came into the room. Aosenla repeated her demand to see the baby and this time, the nurse was ready with an answer. She calmly replied that she was instructed to inform Aosenla that the doctor was doing the rounds and would soon come to her room to talk to her. Aosenla was taken aback by this piece of information and was convinced that there was indeed something seriously wrong with the baby. But she could do nothing about it except wait for the doctor.

It was after nearly an hour that her gynaecologist entered her room and asked her how she was feeling after the operation. Aosenla jerked her head, 'What operation?' and began to once again probe the bandages around her stomach. The doctor gently removed her hands from the operation site and held them in his in order to calm her down. He looked steadily into her troubled eyes and began to speak with as much compassion as he could muster, 'I am afraid I do not have good news for you, madam. You see, by the time it became imperative for us to operate on you in order to try and save both of you, the baby had returned to the horizontal position once again. In the process, there was a tear in the wall of the uterus, and because of the prolonged labour contortions, the umbilical cord got entangled around the neck and he suffocated.' Aosenla interrupted, 'Wait a minute, did you say he?' 'Yes,' the doctor replied, 'There was nothing we could do to revive him and even if we had succeeded, I am afraid his brain would have suffered irreparable damage.'

The stricken mother was looking straight ahead, not seeming to hear what the doctor had just said; concentrating on the unseeing eyes, the doctor pulled his chair closer to the bed and asked, 'Madam, did you understand what I just said? There is no baby now.' After what seemed an age, Aosenla asked, 'Does my husband know about this? What did he say?'

This time it was the doctor's turn to be silent. He looked at her for a long time and when he spoke, there was a slight tremor in the otherwise strong but kind voice. He answered her almost reluctantly, 'He shouted at me and said that I killed his son by my fancy manipulative massages first and then through sheer negligence during the operation. You see, because of your condition, we proceeded slowly with the procedure and maybe lost precious time in extricating the baby before he got entangled in the cord.'

Aosenla did not say anything but continued to gaze up at the ceiling as though she was fascinated by its stark whiteness. At last she spoke, 'Please leave me now, doctor.' But the doctor kept sitting, with his head bowed as if in prayer. After some time he looked up at her with a new resolve in his eyes and said, in a firm voice, 'There is something more that I have to tell you madam.' And seeing the question in her eyes, he continued, 'You see when we were suturing the uterus, we found that there were several tears through which internal fluids had entered. The procedure to clean up and repair all the holes would have taken much time and we realized that if we went ahead with that, your life would have been in great danger. There was no other option for us but to remove it altogether. I am extremely sorry, madam.'

He waited for some kind of reaction like an anguished scream, or a bout of weeping, but neither happened; only a stony silence filled the room. He looked on in great puzzlement at this young woman who had not only lost a much longed-for son but at the same time been told that she could never have another child again. The woman seemed calm, composed and even slightly amused. Her reaction was extraordinary. She looked at the doctor with eyes that seemed to say, 'Thank you for the information you've just given me.' Wordlessly she extended her hand to him in the gesture of farewell. The doctor left, thinking that the natural hysterical reaction to this devastating news would come sooner or later and he reminded himself to instruct the head nurse to keep everything in readiness for such an event.

But the predicted hysteria did not happen at all. Instead, the woman who had suffered this double tragedy seemed to alter in some other way. It was as if an inner force was pushing her to another level of being; she showed definite signs of recovering from both the physical and mental trauma and was responding well to medication. She was once again eating properly and even enjoying the wholesome food that her faithful maid brought from home every day. She wanted to see her daughters but children were not allowed in the hospital; so she had to be content with the messages the maid brought from them.

'Tell mummy we want her home soon,' or 'Does she still remember us?', which made her laugh out loud. Aosenla had plenty of time to contemplate her future. She was disappointed by her husband's apparent reluctance to visit her. In all, he came only three times during her convalescence in the hospital for twelve days, and that too with a friend or two, as if to forestall any private contact with his wife. After a week, he left town on the plea that there were urgent business matters to attend to elsewhere. The mother-in-law however visited her daily and brought assorted cousins and aunts with her, bringing food that she knew Aosenla would never touch: sweet-meats oozing with sugary syrup or hot chutneys unsuitable for her condition. She maintained a pleasant front for all to see but the animated sessions of gossip during those visits were always about women with daughters only and of the fate of these unlucky ones. Aosenla, however, refused to be hurt by the barbs in the seemingly innocuous chatter and often joined in their conversation. The charade continued, it seemed, for everyone's benefit.

The messages from the daughters also continued and now they began to send her lists of what they wanted her to bring for them from the hospital: ribbons, hair clips, crayons and even a pair of high heels for the younger one which made Aosenla laugh. But the next message, 'Ask mummy to bring a nice doll home,' had a different effect on Aosenla; she cried for the first time since her ordeal. Her husband's sudden need to go away on 'business' while she was still in the hospital did not evoke any reaction from her: she was disappointed but merely thought 'how like him to do this' and left it at that. Though most of the time she tried to forget the fact that there was no baby now and that there would never be another, the word 'doll' brought to the fore all her suppressed anguish. Her whole body shook with hoarse sobs and she cried hard and long while the maid turned her face to the wall and wept silent tears in commiseration with her bereaved mistress. When the sobs finally ended, the maid pressed a wet towel to her swollen eyes and face and coaxed her to lie down. She changed the water several times and, wiping out the last tears and smoothing her dishevelled hair, she managed to calm her mistress down. At intervals though, Aosenla would exhale long sob-like sighs as though she was going into another bout of crying. But after a while she seemed to have gained control over her emotions once again and calmly asked the maid to carry a message to her doctor, requesting him to see her after his evening round.

The doctor was a bit late in coming and Aosenla was becoming agitated. The moment he entered the room she demanded in a calm voice to be released that very moment. The doctor was taken aback and started to say something, but the woman cut him short and declared, 'If I am not released immediately, I shall do something drastic for which you will be solely responsible.' He looked around and saw that her belongings were already packed in a suitcase and standing by the door and she was dressed in outdoor clothes. The maid was standing mutely near the suitcase. He turned his gaze to Aosenla and saw the firm resolve in her eyes, but he saw something else also, and began to think that this was the hysteria that he had predicted would come sooner or later. And what if the 'drastic action' she threatened him with was suicidal or something equally violent? The husband's earlier accusation against him still ringing in his ears, the doctor decided that he would not risk any further tangle with this influential family, and, convinced that this was the slow-release hysteria, he decided that it would be better for everyone concerned that this 'unstable' woman be sent home immediately. It was however, no 'hysteria' that had prompted Aosenla to demand to be released in the evening. Ever since the doctor had told her about the baby and her body, she had felt defeated and had been dreading her return to the hostile environment of her home. So she thought that going home in the darkness of the evening would be best. After her bout of crying earlier in the day, she had experienced some relief in her mind and wanted to be home with her daughters as soon as possible.

So Aosenla was officially released and as further wished by her, sent home along with her maid in an ambulance. As she was helped into the vehicle, she turned to the doctor and said in a calm voice, 'Thank you for everything doctor, please send the bill to my husband.' And she was gone. When they were approaching the estate, the driver was instructed to stop by the rear gate of the compound, and the two women alighted and vanished through the gate in the gathering darkness. In contrast with the time when she was transported to the hospital with expectations of coming back with, if not the coveted son, at least a healthy child, her homecoming was stealthy, as though she feared that she would not be allowed through the main gate without a child in her arms and she herself rendered incapable of further procreation. Left to herself, this fact would not have mattered so much; but the moment she set foot in this environment, she knew that she would once again be caught in the undercurrents of the family's displeasure and even accusation that she was responsible for her son's death, thus denying the family the privilege of welcoming a grandson.

8

The mother-in-law was, as expected, peeved that she was not informed about Aosenla's discharge and also that even after she reached home, she did not bother to send any word to her. It was only in the morning when her daughters went to their grandmother's house shouting, 'Granny, granny mummy is home!' that the old woman learnt about the fact. She sulked the whole day and did not come to see her. Only towards evening, she came to Aosenla's house with a bowl of soup, which she dumped unceremoniously on the dining table, and launched straight into a tirade against what she called Aosenla's unseemly behaviour in sneaking into the house.

'What will the people say? The way you discharged yourself and did not even care to inform your own family? If you wanted to disgrace us, you have already accomplished that by the fiasco of your confinement. I had started to feel sorry for you but now I am convinced that God has punished you for your arrogance and willfulness, and you have only to blame yourself for everything that has happened.' Aosenla remained quiet and turned her head on the bed towards the wall. With a loud 'humph' the old woman stamped out of the house.

The news of her coming home must have been flashed to Bendang, wherever he was, and he came home in the afternoon of the next day. Aosenla had dreaded this moment of 'encounter'. But she was in for a pleasant surprise: on seeing her he gave her a tentative smile and, without saying anything, began to unpack his suitcase. First he took out the gifts for his daughters, which were received with shrieks of delight. Next there was a nice shawl for the maid, but the biggest surprise of all was when he took out a beautiful nightgown for her, the very first gift in many a year. Aosenla was stumped for words and she quietly began to cry, seeing which the maid quickly hustled the girls out of the bedroom. They left reluctantly, looking backwards at their father trying to console mummy and leaving in their wake an assortment of wrapping papers, strings and even a slipper. After a while, Aosenla managed to say between her sobs in a small voice, 'I am so sorry.' To which he replied, 'I am sorry too, but more so for you.' She did not know how to take it; did he really mean it? Or did he mean that as far as he was concerned, nothing was lost irretrievably? She simply looked at him with woebegone eyes and tried to read his inner thoughts. For the most part of half an hour, they remained in companionable silence, with an occasional sigh from Aosenla. After a while they heard the patter of small feet, looking for the missing slipper outside the door. When Bendang opened the door, his younger daughter said, 'Cook wants to know what he should make for dinner.' That enquiry somehow restored a semblance of normalcy into the atmosphere, which was threatening to become awkward for everyone. It was however a sombre meal that the family sat through that evening. The girls, sensing the tension still in the air, kept unnaturally quiet and went to bed early on their own.

For the couple too, it was a night fraught with the burden of mutual wariness accumulated through the years, as if one was trying to assess the approachability of the other. There was hardly any meaningful conversation between them except Aosenla's account of her discharge and an apologetic explanation about why she wanted to come home under the cover of darkness. Her husband looked at her long and simply sighed. After a while he said, 'Let's go to bed, I am tired; and so must you be.' Aosenla thought that in his words and gestures, there seemed to be a subtle softening of his attitude towards her, or was she imagining it? She was however still wary and did not want to commit herself to any sort of certainty about her relationship with him; the lesson of the past was still fresh in her mind. The only certainty she had for the moment was that she was strangely content with the present companionship and that she was content to have him home by her side. Long after he started snoring, she lay awake trying to make sense of all that had happened so dramatically; his seeming apathy when she lay in the hospital bed needing the assurance of his care and concern. When she was told about his business trip, her sense of abandonment was acute. But now: how should she take this complete volte-face and show of sympathy, not only for the loss of their son but also of the fact that she was absolutely incapacitated as far as the question of another child was concerned? Her earlier cynicism, she found, was now giving way to a new consideration, almost a new sensation: maybe he too was mourning in his own way and was suffering as much as her. She began to think that the great sense of loss of the much-awaited son and her incapacity to bear any more children was not hers alone. In an almost mute way perhaps her husband was trying to reach out to her and say how sorry he was for this devastating tragedy in their lives. This thought somehow tempered her resentment and anger at the sense of abandonment she had felt at his strange behaviour during the tragic episode. With these hopeful thoughts, she went off to sleep and for the first time in weeks, she slept well and awoke rested and refreshed and in a happy frame of mind.

The morning brought with it the numerous demands of reality diverting her attention to them: the girls had to be dressed for school and their tiffins packed. But first she had to coax them to eat some breakfast, always an ordeal with the younger one. This accomplished, she saw them off with cheery waves, both of them shouting, 'Don't go away again mummy,' which brought back recent memories choking her reply, 'No, I'll be here when you come home.' Next she turned to the larder which needed to be replenished, both hers and Bendang's wardrobes needed to be tidied and the garden needed to be seen to. Applying her mind to all these chores, she felt for the first time perhaps that she was indeed 'needed' then in this family. If not by her husband in the same measure as by her daughters and the household, and she welcomed this sensation with a new awareness of her own self. What she had to do now was to enhance this inner experience to integrate her husband's commitment as well and find a new definition for herself. She began to immerse herself in the recurring and time-consuming household chores as if her life depended upon doing them. The maid protested, asking why madam was unnecessarily wearing herself out when the servants could take care of all the chores. Aosenla merely smiled and did not say anything. After a while even her husband noticed her frenetic activities and told her to slow down but Aosenla replied, 'I am quite recovered now and am happy doing all this; why should I stop?' He merely gave her a puzzled look and did not bring up the topic again.

Though it appeared that Aosenla had put the recent tragedy behind her and was embarking on a new phase of her life, which indeed she was doing, the spectre of death haunted her thoughts all the time. True, she was not a stranger to death; an elder brother had died when she was a small girl and she was inconsolable when they put him in a box before taking him to the cemetery. 'Why?' she had asked again and again, and was told that he would be buried in the ground. Hearing that, she had become hysterical and fought with her mother when the burying party returned to the house. It was the first traumatic experience she had suffered. This death had already become only a faint memory now as she learned to accept and absorb the fact as she grew older. But in the present circumstance, the death of her son sat on her mind like the weight of the whole world on her body, the body which had given him form and life for nine months and had become an inextricable portion of her being. This body of hers now seemed to be detached from her consciousness. His death therefore, constituted not only the wrenching of a vital core of her body but also meant a permanent scarring of her soul. The pain was direct and immediate and was as real as she was alive. All the expectations of holding a living child to her breasts had now become this senseless waste. After the shock of confronting this reality, an immense hollowness settled in the space where her heart was supposed to be. Her body, on the other hand, functioned as if the natural process of birth and all that it entails could not be interfered with, not even by death. Her breasts filled with milk, which became not only a terrible bodily pain but also a recurring reminder of the lost son for whom her body was producing the nourishment. Every time the accumulated milk was suctioned out from her swollen breasts into the waste bin to relieve her of the physical pain, she cried bitterly and cursed her own body for betraying her so cruelly, as though it was mocking her by following its natural rhythm, unmindful of the fact that the child for whom the milk flowed was no longer a part of that life-cycle.

9

Her doctor, in the meantime, was keeping a close watch on her through reports not only from the maid but also from her husband. The doctor had a long discussion with Bendang and expressed his concern about Aosenla's apparent calm, and warned him to be watchful about her behaviour. The doctor was sure that the bereaved woman was fighting her demons by immersing herself in mechanical household chores while, he said, she was seething inside with the great unshared grief. He was afraid, he added, that Aosenla might suffer a nervous breakdown if she continued in this frenetic manner over trivial chores.

Bendang was visibly alarmed and requested the doctor to visit them more often so that he could assess her condition and determine for himself whether he was right about his prognosis rather than basing his opinion on reports alone. So a new phase in the doctor-patient relationship began. Whenever he could spare some time, the kindly doctor, named Kilangtemjen or Kilang for short, began to visit their home. On occasions when Bendang happened to be out, he sat on the verandah with Aosenla sipping cups of tea and observing her actions and general behaviour carefully, trying at the same time to maintain a casual manner as one would during a social visit. To his own amazement, Kilang began to see that this Aosenla was more relaxed than the woman he always thought of as his patient. She seemed to be at ease not only with him but also with her circumstances. So he too became less formal with her and volunteered information about his family and work. Sometimes he would talk about his involvement with an NGO, which gave shelter to orphans, abandoned children from broken homes and battered women. This particular information perked Aosenla up visibly; it seemed to strike a chord with her and she began to question him closely about the extent of his work in the destitute home simply called the Home: how it was funded, who the workers were and how many women and children were sheltered there. And she enquired whether the government had any interest or responsibility in the functioning of the home. To this question, Kilang first gave a derisive snort and said, 'Huh! You expect the present government to give a damn, (sorry), about these unfortunates? Instead, they tried to dissuade me from involving myself with the NGO because, they said, all these destitutes are lazy good-for-nothings of loose character, and told me that the government cannot help because there was no budgetary allocation for such homes. It was also hinted that I should not be seen spending more time there and neglecting my government job in the hospital. I ask you what do they know about the suffering of these women and children? But let me not bore you with my extracurricular preoccupations. I am your doctor and I want to see you fully recovered from your ordeal. So take care of your diet and do not overtire yourself with household chores, there are enough people to do that.' As he rose to go, he looked deeply into her eyes and said, 'Madam, you have my deepest sympathy and also my admiration for the way you have endured the pain and anguish of these past months. Anything you need, even if it is only to talk, do not hesitate, just call me and I will be here, any time, any time at all.'

After this particular visit of the doctor, Aosenla became pensive and began to think of how the others might be viewing her recent behaviour. She decided to take his advice about not overexerting and gradually relegated most of the housework to the servants. But she still supervised her daughters' food, clothes, and homework, bath-time and bedtime rituals. It gave her more time to be with them and in the process made her an indispensable part of their growing up. It amazed her to see how fast they were outgrowing their things: shoes, dresses and blazers. Remembering the doctor's talk about the Home, she began to store the girls' discarded things in an old suitcase. The maid was surprised; earlier, these would have been divided between her, the cook and the gardener and sometimes even the handyman would get some things, which the others did not fancy. But now, she decided, madam was becoming stingier and she did not like it one bit.

Though the two daughters were too young to fully grasp the ramifications of the recent tragedy that had befallen the family, Chubala, the older one, was burning inside with the question regarding the absence of a child when the mother returned from the hospital in the dark of the night. There were many occasions when she nearly blurted out the question at her mother. But an inner voice always cautioned her to wait a little longer. It so happened that one morning she woke up in a terrible mood; she could not pinpoint any physical ailment but she decided that she would not go to school that day and confront her mother with the question. So she declared that she had an upset tummy and begged to be allowed to rest at home. Though Aosenla was a bit skeptical, the father looked at his elder daughter and saw the desperate plea in her eyes and said that she could stay back for today. So once more she got under the quilt and pretended to go to sleep.

After the younger girl was seen off to school with a long face because she too had wanted to stay back, the mother returned to the morning rituals of preparing her husband's bath and clothes and saw to his breakfast. Only after he left, she went into her daughters' room to check on Chubala whom she found sitting up with a glum face. She became anxious and moving nearer put a hand on her temple asking, 'What's wrong baby, do you have a fever? Or is your stomach hurting you more?'

The daughter remained silent and only glared at her mother with so much intensity that Aosenla literally took a step back. She was getting frightened by her daughter's behaviour and wanted to call her maid. But she could not do anything, she just stayed rooted to the spot near the bed. Seeing her mother's reaction, Chubala lowered her eyes and in a timid voice, said, 'Mummy, I want ask you a question. Will you tell me the truth?'

The mother stammered, 'Yes' and sat on the edge of the bed. After gazing at her mother for a long while, the daughter blurted out her question, 'Where did you leave the baby? Why did you come home alone? Is it because it was another girl? Or is it because grandma did not want another girl?'

Aosenla was completely taken aback and stunned by the force of these questions, which almost sounded like accusations, and for quite some time, she remained mute before the force of their anger. She realized her daughter was also in some form of mourning for the absence of another child for which her mother had gone to the hospital in the first place. The mother edged closer and held her daughter in her arms and began to sob. Realizing that it was her questions that had brought on the tears, Chubala also began to sob loudly and rocked her frail mother, as a mother would do for a daughter.

After the bout of sobbing subsided for both, Aosenla went to the bathroom and came out with a wet towel and wiped her daughter's face; the daughter did the same for her mother. In that instant of mutual ministering, it seemed that a new understanding dawned on both of them and a fresh bond was forged between mother and daughter, and Aosenla experienced an inner peace not felt in a long while. She looked at her young daughter and realized how sensitive her daughter had become to the inner turmoil that the mother was going through for the last months, and in spite of her best efforts at hiding her true emotions from everyone in the family, Chubala had mistakenly interpreted her mother's behaviour as her sense of guilt for not bringing a baby home. Emitting a heavy sigh, Aosenla hugged her daughter close to her and began to speak in a small voice. She explained why she had to come home without their brother because he did not survive the ordeal of being born and that the doctors and nurses, and in fact nobody could have done anything to avoid the tragedy. After the narration, Aosenla said to her daughter in a very calm voice, 'You know Chuba, in life many things happen contrary to our wishes and the sooner you accept this fact, the happier you will be.' Her daughter came closer to her mother and hugged her tightly and with sobs in her voice said how much she loved and admired her mother. And after a little while she added, 'Mommy, I am sorry for my harsh words to you earlier, please forgive me.' And before the mother could say anything, she hurriedly added, 'I hope daddy also understands you like I do.' So saying Chubala once again disappeared into the bathroom, leaving the mother to mull over what had transpired in the last half hour between mother and daughter. These words, coming from the mouth of her innocent daughter, were like a fresh wave of inner hope for Aosenla and she resolved that whatever happened now, she would cherish this momentous encounter and dedicate all her efforts towards building a happy home for her girls.

Aosenla had held off talking about the Home with Bendang for many weeks. She was unsure as yet where she stood in his scheme of things and how he would react if she showed any interest in this kind of organization. But she dreaded her mother-in-law's reaction most of all. As it was, she was now almost a persona non grata in the family and the people from the big house could hardly keep a civil tongue even in the presence of family and relatives. What the mother-in-law said in private, and which was somehow conveyed to Aosenla, did not bear repeating. But by now she had become indifferent to many of the things that had earlier caused so much anguish, especially after her heart-to-heart conversation with her daughter. In an inexplicable way, the tragedy seemed to have aroused a toughness in her that she was not aware of possessing. Instead of being apologetic and timid, she assumed a 'couldn't-care-less' attitude, which surprised even her. It was almost like saying, 'It is my life and I am going to lead it in the way I want to.' And she was certain that Bendang had noticed this streak of resilience in her and somehow he too seemed to have grown more mellow and more courteous towards her. But she wondered if the softening she saw in her husband's attitude would make him amenable to what she planned on asking him. Would he agree to her proposal to involve herself in charity work in the Home, that too, so soon after her ordeal?

The opportunity to broach the subject presented itself in the form of a news item in the local daily about the suicide bid of one of the inmates of the Home. As luck would have it, Bendang was home at teatime. The family was having their repast on the verandah after the girls came home from school and were clamouring for the father's attention with stories about their day. Bendang listened to his daughters for some time; both of them were talking at the same time and trying to outshout the other, which became too much for him. He put his fingers in his ears and grimaced. This was the moment Aosenla was waiting for. She gathered them in her arms and said, 'Don't you see what daddy is saying? He is saying enough, so like good girls leave us now and see what ayah is doing to your dolls.' At this, the girls shrieked and dashed into the house to rescue their 'babies'. Bendang looked at his wife and said, 'Clever; was there anything you wanted to say to me in private?' At this, Aosenla blushed and said to herself, 'How transparent can I be?' Keeping a calm exterior she began to talk about the Home run by Kilang and his friends and expressed her wish to devote a few hours there to help out by talking to the women and children. She also told him about the used clothes she had kept aside to donate to the Home. Bendang looked incredulous at first and then annoyed at being caught so off-guard. What the doctor had told him about his wife's suppressed emotions leading to a severe post-natal depression was very far from what she was proposing to do. It was not at all the kind of thinking he would associate with her present state of mind. He realized he could say nothing at this moment of disjunct and, mumbling about some 'later discussion', he almost ran into the house. Aosenla continued to sit there forlorn, convinced that he would never allow her to have any direct involvement with the affairs of the Home. She felt terribly disappointed and mumbled to herself, over and over, 'All I want is to help those less fortunate than us.' After a while she heard Bendang start his jeep and zoom out of the compound in the gathering dusk.

As he drove out of the compound, Bendang was wondering what had prompted his wife to come out with this absurd request: his wife going out to 'work' and that too in the Home. Didn't she know what the townspeople thought of the inmates?

The 'later discussion' of course did not take place, but Aosenla was not deterred; it merely made her more determined to not give up without a fight. She had however learnt by this time that she would never have her way by being aggressive or petulant; she knew her husband quite well by now. So she did not mention the subject again at all. Instead she began to go out to friends' and relatives' houses for visits and invited them home for tea or lunch and sometimes even lavish dinners. Her daughters were also encouraged to bring their friends home and soon even the parents began to be included in birthday parties. Thus began a hectic cycle of social visits and return visits and Aosenla's social circle was expanding rapidly. The shy timid girl before the third pregnancy seemed to have emerged out of a cocoon, as it were, and was turning out to be quite a personality in her own right.

This was something which astounded her husband and his family; they could not imagine how this poor little girl generally considered of no social consequence earlier was now being made welcome in the best homes in town. Her mother-in-law, who was watching her comings and goings closely, could not contain her anger at being upstaged by this 'nobody' and began once again to provoke Bendang by ridiculing him and saying that he had lost all control over his wife. He was at first annoyed by his mother's interference in his family affairs but he too began to observe his wife more critically now. It was true that earlier, the woman who was earlier merely his shadow, was now creating an identity of her own and was beginning to acquire a new status among his friends too. She was now being considered for important positions in civic organizations. For example, when a group of influential women got together to form a Mothers' Union, the unanimous choice for president was Aosenla. She was also inducted into the governing body of her daughters' school. She was becoming quite an important person indeed. What galled Bendang most was the fact that Aosenla did not consult him about accepting or not accepting the offers. It was like telling him that she no longer needed his permission or approval to go out of the home and render her services to society.

If others, including her husband and his family, saw her as such, Aosenla was clear in her mind that whatever she was doing was absolutely out of her conviction that if she was to gain any control of her own life, the process had to begin at home; she needed to ensure that Bendang accepted the fact that she was no longer merely his shadow, and that she had to have a say in what she wanted to do with her time and life. The subtle power play that was unfolding before his eyes jolted Bendang out of his complacency. When he looked back at the episode when he and his family tried to cow her down almost to the point of erasing her self-identity, she had fallen back on her cultural superiority and the moral strength of her innocence to defeat their attempt. Once again he was being put in the same position of disadvantage by her clever move of going out of the home environment and successfully creating a legitimate space for herself in the social arena. This time round he could not manoeuvre her sexuality to subdue her physically; recent events had ensured this could no longer happen. He began to feel helpless and resented the fact that it was Aosenla who had outsmarted him; he resolved he would find ways to clip her new-found wings. Others outside the family circle, however, saw Aosenla's social activities as noble and even heroic after her great ordeal, and expressed their admiration for her.

10

In the meantime, Aosenla started inviting Kilang and his family to her parties, which she organized frequently. The kindly doctor was intrigued at first; he thought that it was yet another tactic the woman was employing to keep her emotions at bay. He still believed that her suppressed feelings would one day erupt in the form of a huge hysterical outburst. But he went along, if only to humour his patient and to make sure her emotional equilibrium remained stable. But what he saw in her public persona puzzled him no end. She seemed to be perfectly at ease, not only with others but with herself too. She was even beginning to laugh at herself publicly at times, recalling certain incidents from the past to show what a fool she was to have done something or to have believed something so obviously outlandish. And she would turn to Bendang and ask coyly, 'Isn't that true darling?' putting her husband in an utterly uncomfortable position. After attending a few of these parties, Kilang was convinced that Aosenla's vision lay elsewhere, beyond merely discomfiting her husband. The more he pondered over this, the more convinced he became that she was merely using this strategy to achieve something bigger, and he began to question his own simplistic prognosis about a complicated marvel like a woman's psyche.

If the public performances projected her as the perfectly

adjusted woman after the tragedy, it was quite another story for the real Aosenla. Safe within the privacy of her home, she often experienced an extraordinary sensation: during these spells she felt that she was there and not there at all at the same time. It was as if the fluttering, busy housewife and the emerging socialite were two totally different beings and that she was watching them from a great distance with puzzled amusement. They seemed to belong to two contrasting realms: the frenzied activities of the physical self and the convoluted workings of an inner consciousness. Not only that, the acute sense of detachment was also evident in her intimate relationship with her husband. During their occasional lovemaking, Aosenla felt totally removed from the act she was participating in; sometimes she would cold-bloodedly watch her husband's grimaced exertions as he strove to climax and inwardly jeer at him for the sheer futility of his efforts. It did not matter to her whether the man knew the thoughts in the inert body lying beneath him. She merely accepted these encounters as one more absurdity to contend with. But whenever he tried to kiss her, she would deliberately turn her face away to avoid contact because she felt that a kiss was much more personal and intimate than allowing him to exert himself over a prostrate body from which the mind had already fled. Her mental non-involvement in the act was like sacrificing a half-dead animal in a perfunctory ritual of appeasement at the altar of a stone-god of an obsolete religion. At the same time she also knew that it was a surrender of sorts, but she believed that it was a strategic surrender. She wanted to keep him 'not hungry' in that way but denied him the intimacy of a kiss in order to keep a deeper core of herself inviolate.

This was a new phase, as far as Aosenla was concerned, in her physical relationship with her husband. In the beginning she had accepted the sexual act as normal: the husband had a right to her body and as a wife she had an obligation to yield to him. Apart from this 'legal' interpretation, she mistakenly believed that he would also learn to love her in the way that she interpreted the word. What she did not realize then was that for him, she was his 'property' and he could do whatever he liked with her body. It was only now that Aosenla understood the full implications of some early incidents when he demonstrated this fact, though she was much too engrossed in her own make-believe world to see them for what they actually were. She now remembered one particular incident of this early period. She was a very private person and extremely shy about baring her body even before her husband. So she preferred making love in total darkness and was never fully naked in his presence. Bendang was amused at first, and he went along with her wishes. But as time went on, he became more demanding and aggressive during these physical encounters. Once, when he was in a slightly drunken and belligerent mood, he ordered her to remove every stitch of clothing from her body. When she demurred, he yelled at her and forcefully accomplished the job himself. He then put on every light in the room and set the player at full volume, after which he pushed her on to the bed and proceeded to take the totally naked and terrified woman with such violent exertions that she began to wonder if the liquor had addled his brain. After much effort he exploded into her with a loud and hoarse animal-like groan. Aosenla was totally taken aback by this wild ferocity; she lay inert beneath him for some time and when it seemed prudent, quietly crawled out from under the sweaty and spent body now giving way to the beginning of a disgusting snore. She rushed to the bathroom and washed herself angrily and vigorously as though she wanted to cleanse herself of all the impurity that had been forced into her. It was a nightmarish experience that stayed with Aosenla for a very long time. But strangely, at that point of time, it never occurred to her that he had committed any offence against her. She simply thought that he was only exercising his prerogative as a husband, though she had wished, for a tiny moment, that he could have been a little gentler. Two days after this, Bendang decided to go on another business trip out of town. Aosenla remembered this particular day because it happened to be her birthday; she had pleaded with him to postpone his trip by a day so that the family could enjoy a quiet birthday dinner but he simply gave her a funny look and stepped out of the house. She could not say what she had expected him to do; stay back and apologize for his cruelty on the marriage bed? She would never know.

But he did a curious thing: he left a birthday present for her with the maid. When the maid brought it to her after his departure, Aosenla was in two minds: should she accept it or should she ask the maid to give it back to the master when he came home? But she did not want the maid to be privy to any sign of discord between them because she knew that the knowledge would soon spread among all the servants and would instantly reach the big house too. Besides, after a while, curiosity got the better of her and she took it and ordered the maid out of the room. Inside the ordinary packaging, there was an elegant leather case, inside which there reposed a beautiful gold chain on a red velvet bed. Looking closely she saw that the exquisite pendant had her initials in tiny diamonds. Aosenla was taken aback; what was the meaning of this? Why did he leave it with the maid? Why didn't he give it to her himself? What was he trying to say? Was it his apology for what he did to her two nights ago? Though these were perplexing questions and she was unsure of the answers, she knew one thing for certain: she would never wear that chain. She closed the case and once again putting it inside the brown outer wrapping, deposited it in the old jewellery box where she put all her discarded trinkets. If Bendang had expected a 'thank you' for his gift he never got it; nor did he indicate any curiosity about its fate. Also, if he felt any resentment at the summary rejection he never showed it either.

Though she remembered this incident with new understanding now, Aosenla did not want to think about the earlier phase of her physical relationship with her husband when the third pregnancy had occurred because of the role she had played in it. But in the present context, she was fully aware that she was deliberately playing the role of a dispassionate manipulator, a total reversal of their earlier positions. And the wonder of it all was that she did not feel even an iota of guilt or remorse. She also could not say whether Bendang had done what he did to her body even in other earlier incidents, as a deliberate attempt to hurt her. Was the aggression, she wondered, a spontaneous reaction on account of some fixed idea in his mind that it was the only way through which he could establish his dominion over her? Did he recognize some inner resistance in her and somehow felt threatened by it? She would never know. But as for herself, she felt certain that she had indeed entered a new phase of her life where she would be able to assert her true self.

11

The so-called business trips had often been Bendang's way of running away from real or imagined crises in his life. The sense of unease that began in his mind, since his initial meeting with Aosenla on her uncle's bamboo platform before their marriage, had never quite gone away. It lay there like an irritating welt that would at times subside and at other times threaten to fester into a gaping wound. Several times in the last years, he had tried to ask himself why it should be so, but each time he would be overwhelmed by his inability to fathom the inner depths of this girl, now grown into a poised woman who had survived the onslaughts of his private aggression and the outward hostility of his mother and sisters. Her indomitable spirit had some indefinable clout over his outward bluster of masculinity and superiority. Take for instance the most recent encounter in bed; why had he become so savage in his taking of her body? He tried to reconstruct the events: what had she said when he asked her to undress? Was she defiant, did she look intimidated? He could not remember now; he only remembered that he was a little drunk; in fact had been drinking with his cronies where the talk invariably drifted towards women's bodies and the usual boasts of drunks about the various women they had had over the years. And then in a flash it came to him; following the drift of their conversation he remembered that he had realized that he'd never seen Aosenla completely naked before and this made him feel unequal to his peers and listening to their tales of conquest, he immediately thought of this as a drawback in his sexual relationship with his own wife. He had therefore hurried home and had initiated the aggression not only on her body but also on their fragile relationship. The recollection of his irrational act was so sudden and jolting that he had to stop the car in order to control his agitation.

He got out of the vehicle and sat under a bush and ordered his handyman to pour a cup of tea from the flask that he always carried. After the tea and a cigarette, he asked the boy, who was also an expert driver, to take over and Bendang sat in the back with his reflections. This time around he began to question himself why he had left the gift with the maid. Couldn't he have given it to Aosenla himself? What did she think of it, because he knew that by now the maid must have given it to her mistress as instructed by him? But the most important question was why had he acted so out of character by buying the expensive gift in the first place? Then he remembered that actually, the gift had been purchased during Aosenla's first pregnancy and hoping that the child would be a male, Bendang had planned on giving it to her after the delivery during the celebrations. Holding back the gift in itself was mean; he now realized and wished that he had given it to her many years ago. But earlier he had never felt the need for an overt gesture of friendliness or even 'reconciliation' of any sort as he now did after his most recent shameful behaviour towards her. He had almost forgotten it as it lay in the secret compartment of his desk-drawer these many years. It was only when he was overtaken by a strong sense of remorse after assaulting her and was beginning to think of ways to make amends with her that he remembered it. So the gift, which was initially to have been in celebration, had thus been turned into a symbol of abject apology, though the ostensible reason here was her birthday. But even in this gesture, he seemed to have failed to convey his honest feelings to her personally. Because of this history behind the gift, and his overwhelming sense of guilt, he could not muster enough moral courage to present it to her himself before he left the house. By delegating the task to the maid, Bendang had once again stripped the gift of any real significance; it would now remain only an unmentionable 'thing' between them.

Normally Bendang enjoyed his trips out of town; the drive through forested roads, the quaint tea-shops where he and his companions sat and chatted with other travellers always made him happy. But on this particular trip, he could not erase the sense of shame and remorse for what he had done to his wife. He berated himself for being the coward that he was and became increasingly angry with himself for having allowed the bawdy remarks of his drinking cronies to dictate his behaviour. For the first time in his adult life, Bendang was giving in to this rare introspection and what he saw in himself made him cringe. His mood swung from bad to morose, and on the outskirts of their destination town, he ordered the driver to turn, saying he was not feeling well and they headed home. Aosenla was mildly surprised when her husband reached home, but without showing much emotion, she saw to his bath and dinner and allowed the girls to stay with their father much longer than usual before they were gently ushered into their own beds. Bendang tried to figure out whether Aosenla had seen the gift and waited eagerly for her reaction. But none was forthcoming even though she knew that he expected her acknowledgement. Both strove for a normalcy that initially precluded words or touch, but in the end it was Aosenla who gave in seeing the man's obvious distress and offered to massage his aching head. He looked at her with surprise, his delight apparent in his eyes. But he knew that he had to be content with the present offer. A little reluctantly but nevertheless gratefully, he submitted to the soothing touch of her gentle fingers.

The quality in Aosenla that Bendang was unable to fathom so far was her innate reticence, which abhorred all forms of confrontation, a quality that was often mistaken for timidity. But gradually he was beginning to recognize this aspect of her character as some form of resistance and was therefore wary of her when she withdrew into these periodic spells of isolating herself not only from him but from the girls as well. In spite of this, she generally seemed calm and calculating in her intimate relations with her husband, but there were times during such periods that Aosenla strangely felt as if she was losing her grip on the reality outside the bedroom. On some days she would feel weightless and had the sensation that she was floating in the air. During these moments she would see the furniture, clothes and even the vegetables from her kitchen swirling around her. And afterwards she would feel dizzy and had to lie down to calm her nerves. This phase however did not last long because she instinctively knew that sooner or later the 'floating' self had to come back to the world of the 'watchful' self and that it was this actual self who had to chart a new course of life. But how was she to achieve this? And more importantly, she asked herself the question, why was she behaving and thinking in this manner? She pondered long over this during the afternoons when the children were away at school and Bendang was either out or busy with his business matters. She realized that these delusional periods in her mind started after Bendang dismissed her wish to help out in Dr. Kilang's Home and her inability to assert her will on the issue. And now she was asking herself: why could she not bring up the subject for discussion with him again?

Take him up on the 'later discussion' he had mumbled the first time she mentioned it? What was she afraid of? The more she thought about it, the more convinced she became that 'being afraid' was a condition of her mind since her marriage when she discovered that her 'unequal' status had kept her suppressed not only by her husband but also by his entire family. It was a position from which she had not moved and therefore was unable to become 'unafraid'. It was an extremely painful realization and she brooded over this for days, but concluded that she was not yet ready to take a decisive step to free herself from this self-doubt. Unlike the public persona she had assumed lately, Aosenla was still reticent about openly contesting her husband's will and inwardly suffered on that account.

On some other days when her mind was not too agitated, she would recall the most important events in her married life: the birth of her daughters. The first child was born only after two years of her marriage. When she did not conceive immediately, the women in the family, especially her mother-in-law, began to speculate if there was any history of barrenness in her family, or if there was something wrong with her because in school she was active in games like basketball, long jump and other games. But the newly wedded Aosenla was totally oblivious to all this speculation and was in a world of her own, the centre of which was her husband Bendang. There was great jubilation when she conceived and the general expectation was that it was surely going to be a boy. In traditional households there were so many taboos regarding the diet of pregnant women. Eating bitter and sour vegetables and fruits were considered bad for the growing child. She was told that in their village, pregnant women developed a craze for a certain kind of loose stone and would flock to the place from where it could be dug. They wanted to bring that for her from the village if she was interested! And the role of dreams! Rural folk lay a great deal of emphasis on dreams and their interpretations for the conduct of their lives. So the father-in-law began to talk about his dreams, the interpretations of which all indicated that Aosenla was going to give birth to a boy because he dreamt only of spears, daos and the like because all these implements were associated with males!

She was pampered throughout the first pregnancy and there was a general air of great expectancy. And when the labour pains started in the middle of the night, the patriarch insisted that the confinement would be at home and ordered that a lady doctor and a staff nurse be brought from the government hospital to supervise the delivery. But when, after nearly twelve hours, the child turned out to be a girl, the family did their best not to show any disappointment openly and consoled themselves by saying that Aosenla still had many childbearing years to produce sons. According to custom the paternal grandfather had to suggest a name and he chose the name Chubarenla, which means 'royal increase', indicating the family's status. After all, whether a boy or a girl, this child belonged to their family and must be acknowledged in a befitting manner by giving her a royal name.

What she remembered of the first childbirth was mostly the pain when the contractions began. Recalling the acute pains of childbirth, she now understood that this was an experience that only a woman's body had to endure; no power on earth could alleviate it or make it go away. Pain was the price a woman had to pay in order to become a mother. She remembered screaming and howling at the severest contractions during the long process of birthing and begging for pain-killers from the doctor who tried to soothe her by saying, 'Very soon now, I can feel the head way down. Push, push hard when the pain starts.' Aosenla got angry and felt like kicking the nurse hovering around with a wet towel and wiping her sweaty brows. Just then an enormous darkness seemed to overwhelm her and, uttering an unearthly scream, she bore down hard when she heard a collective sigh and exclamations, 'There, there it's out.' As she drifted into an exhausted oblivion, her last thought was one of gratitude only because the pain had gone. The relief was short-lived when she saw the disappointed look on her mother-in-law's face, but she did not care. As she held her new-born in her arms, she felt exultant and said to herself, 'There, I've done it; I have given birth to another human being.' The pain that she had suffered so recently got pushed back in her consciousness as she looked at the perfectly formed baby sleeping in the folds of soft flannels close to her. She recalled the delight and wonder when it was confirmed that she was pregnant. And now she felt a sense of accomplishment as she held the tiny wonder in her arms and hoped that the child would bring her husband closer to her. It did not matter that it was a girl; she was theirs.

When she got pregnant the first time, Aosenla had no inkling of the kind of pain that a woman has to endure at childbirth and was therefore full of happy thoughts. The second time around however, her thoughts were of a different kind. She dreaded the pains and hoped fervently that the second child would be a boy so that she would be spared the accusing looks of the family she had seen the first time. Her second child was born within eighteen months of the first and Aosenla did not know how to cope with the tremendous changes taking place in her life so rapidly. First there were the long faces around her bed after the baby was born. After the baby was cleaned and dressed, the nurse put the baby by her side and without a word left the room. The undeclared antagonism must have been sensed by the baby, because it cried a lot and refused to suckle. And this time even Bendang could not hide his disappointment at the birth of another girl. Aosenla had to bear the silent accusations as if it was her fault that the baby was a girl. The father-in-law in the meantime had to name this baby also but did not come himself like the first time and instead sent the name through his oldest son-in-law. He was a kindly man and, calling Bendang into the room, said, 'The grandfather asked me to tell you that this child should be named Tianaro,' which means 'fortune's flower'. A good name, but Aosenla knew that the diminutive would be Narola, a flower and which had nothing royal about it.

12

The tragedy of the third confinement was a totally different story and perhaps subconsciously, Aosenla tried to relegate it to the back of her mind. She knew that if she were to succeed in this, she had to concentrate on the living and the present situation; the past had to be kept at bay. As she now immersed herself in caring for the girls and the household in general, she realized that it was a good strategy, one that could help her to establish an equilibrium for herself. She found that these moments of introspection were good for her and she felt herself becoming more resilient because she had accepted all that had happened in her life so far.

She realized too that in spite of her growing alienation from her husband, she had experienced a great sense of fulfilment after the birth of her two daughters. She believed that life had acquired a new meaning through their entry into the immediate and most personal circle of her existence. She was now 'needed' if not by her husband, at least by her daughters and this was a novel experience for her. Before their birth she had merely existed as Bendang's shadow and he had never admitted to needing her, except as a complement to his social image. And of course there was this almost casual 'taking' of his rightful dues from her body. Motherhood had ushered in a new awareness in Aosenla's mind: her responsibility now was not only to nurture her marriage for form's sake but more importantly, to create a real home for her daughters.

As she recalled the pain of two childbirths, Aosenla began to mull over the nature of that pain. Though all living beings are subject to pain at some time or other, she thought, birth pangs were borne only by the female of the species. No wonder then that even language, in its own way captures the essence of this particular pain: the birth of a child is often described as 'so and so has been delivered of a child'. At the end of the pain, she thought, there is indeed deliverance, not only from the pains but also from being encumbered with another life within the body.

Aosenla recalled the moment when her first child was pushed out of her body. She found it difficult to describe the pain when the process was on; but when it reached its peak with the final exhalation and the child emerged from the dark canal, it was excruciating. The aftermath, though, was something which she could only describe as 'sublime' because her body had given life to another human being, a feat that no male could ever experience.

She thought too about all the problems that had accompanied the third pregnancy. First there were the particular circumstance of conception, which Aosenla considered to be fraught with deceit on both sides. Then all the actual physical problems, which ended so tragically in the death of the much-awaited son. She also had to bear her mother-in-law's taunts and barbs all the time. One afternoon as she sat in her usual chair in the garden, she heard her mother-in-law talking loudly to a relative who had come to visit.

'See, there she is, she sits like that every day, does not talk to us any more. I don't know what has happened to her - maybe she is worried that the baby will turn out to be another girl this time too. But you know Bendang's father dreamt last night that he was sharpening a dao and he said that it was a very good omen. He is confident that it is going to be a boy, he has enough granddaughters.' Then in a loud voice, she began to talk about a woman in the village who had given birth to five daughters. The other woman responded, 'Yes, I remember vaguely, we were quite young then, but what happened?' 'Don't you remember?' the old woman replied, 'She was divorced and the man took another wife. The second wife also gave birth to two girls first and then a son.'

Aosenla knew that the old woman had meant for her to hear what they were discussing. As she sat there listening to the barbed comments, she wondered: would Bendang also be so desperate for a son that he would be willing to look for another wife? But as soon as the thought came into her mind, she berated herself, 'Hold on, this is the twentieth century and I am no village woman. Besides, it is the man who is responsible for the sex of the child.' But to whom could she say this - her husband, his mother, the relative or to herself? Didn't she also secretly long for a son, if only to stop her mother-in-law's spiteful remarks? And the supreme irony of her life was that she nearly died giving birth to the much-desired son, only to lose him.

But gradually, Aosenla began to realize that dwelling on the past served no purpose; such thoughts only aggravated her inner turmoil, and threatened to blur her sense of reality. She told herself that if she were to overcome these moods, she had to fall back on her own resources. She knew that there was an inner strength in her and she decided to take control of her life and set her priorities right. After the traumatic events surrounding her third childbirth, Aosenla's concerns about 'nurturing' her marriage were now almost subsumed by her resolve to create a real home for her daughters where her husband might or might not have a role to play. But of one thing she was sure: she had to create a world for herself too in the process, with or without him. 'With or without' was a revolutionary phrase even to her own self; could she, the timid Aosenla, translate this resolve into action? Life had taken a different turn for her and she knew she was no longer that person who had preferred to remain in the shadow of the man the world knew as her husband. She knew, without malice or rancor, that the gulf between them had somehow widened.

She felt the loss of her child acutely, for he had been nourished by the life force within her. The fact that she had also nearly died in the process only accentuated the tragedy. If the husband shared the grief of the double tragedy, there was no visible indication of it. But deep in her mind, Aosenla knew that to think that her husband was immune to such feelings would be to deny him his basic humanity. She knew this rationally but if she still harboured any resentment towards him, it was simply on a person-to-person basis. To mitigate the pain of her loss and her sense of acute abandonment by him, Aosenla turned all her attention to her living children. Any observer would have accepted the fact as only natural. What they did not know was that when Aosenla immersed herself in her daughters' lives, it was for her a deliberate and convenient way to move as far away as possible from any emotional involvement and physical contact with her husband. This helped her to release a positive energy and to come out of her emotional isolation. She also discovered that maternal love was strong, fulfilling and free. She discovered a new self as a mother. Her renewed involvement with her children gave her a fresh sense of responsibility not merely for their physical well-being but also in shaping their view of the world. She often told them about the hardships of her childhood, and how she had tried to overcome this handicap by excelling in her studies.

One day, her elder daughter Chubala piped up, 'So, since we have no problems like you, we need not try too hard, isn't that right mummy?' Aosenla replied, 'No my dear girl, you will have to work hard because we both want to see you do well in life and that can be done only through your own merit, not by what your parents are. I was trying to compensate a social handicap but for you, you'd be building on what you already have in your family. '

The younger one quietly snuggled up to her mother, 'Mummy, all that I want is for you to stay with us all the time and never go away. And I will prove to you that I can beat Hekali this time and get the first position in the finals.' The mother gathered them both in her arms and rocked gently in the warmth of their togetherness.

Sometimes Bendang would join them when he heard the three of them chatting and laughing as if by entering their circle he was trying to remind Aosenla that he too was a part of their lives. On such occasions, she would turn her attention to him and watch his wistful eyes as he surveyed the faces of his daughters. At these times she would wonder if he was thinking of what might have been if their son had survived and if he still blamed her for that. Or had he passed that stage and was he reaching out to express his need for them? In the early days, he had seemed to be so self-sufficient, arrogant and almost indifferent. Could that man be the same Bendang who now seemed to be humbling himself before her? She could not decide whether to take this change at face value or still maintain a watchful cynicism towards him as she had been doing so far. But at least for the sake of her daughters, she tried to involve him in their activities like going on picnics or to their friends' parties. Once they all went to the town's only cinema hall to see a movie but the projector broke down so many times that they decided to leave before the interval and came home disappointed. Afterwards of course, the girls would recall how the figures looked just before a breakdown and exaggerate their features and burst into peals of laughter at the recollection.

The spontaneous openness with which Aosenla dealt with her daughters was a contrast to the way in which she seemed to accept Bendang's overtures of truce. She would occasionally lapse into her regressive moods when she was with him, allowing herself to go along with whatever he wished to do. She no longer waited up for him even if he was late by only half an hour for meals. She would stamp her feet and mutter angry words if he was late getting dressed to go to church or parties. But she was no longer solicitous about his clothes when he had to go out of town; she left all these to her maid. Buttons missing from his shirts or jackets were no longer a concern for her, nor whether his shoes were polished or if his socks matched. These mundane everyday housewifely chores were a thing of the past as far as she was concerned. But she was very particular about her daughters' grooming; she supervised everything that concerned them and would scold the servants if even a strand of hair were out of place. Her distancing of herself from her husband was becoming more pronounced by the day. The servants too began to notice this, and their backroom chats were showing signs of resentment at her 'cruelty' towards her husband. During quiet moments, Aosenla sometimes wondered if her daughters noticed her indifference towards their father.

Bendang too had noticed her deliberate withdrawal from him, but he was doing his best to hide it. Inwardly though, he was hurt and concerned. He began to think of ways to placate her and proposed that just the two of them go away for a vacation to Darjeeling. He was convinced that his wife, who had not travelled outside the state, would be overjoyed at the prospect. Aosenla, however, was non-committal, and merely asked who would look after the girls. Bendang's answer was, 'They are old enough now, and my mother is in the same compound. She will gladly supervise the running of the household and the girls' homework.' Still, his wife remained indifferent.

Next, he enlisted the help of Kilang in trying to persuade Aosenla. The doctor was not willing to interfere in their family matters, but Bendang insisted and so the next evening he came to visit them as usual. Over drinks, the conversation turned to vacations and Bendang, as if on cue, told Kilang, 'You see doctor, I have been trying to persuade Asen to go away for a vacation with me. But she is reluctant to leave the girls. She also says that she does not feel up to it. Now you tell me, is she not fit enough to travel?' At this remark, Aosenla seemed to snap out of a trance and before the doctor could reply, she spoke up, 'Of course I am fit enough to travel and Bendang, did I absolutely say no?' Kilang did not know what to say, he simply smiled and said, 'It seems settled then. Have a wonderful vacation.' As he drove home, he chuckled to himself, thinking that his presence was not necessary at all; everything fell into place and the vacation that Bendang was planning for was a fait accompli.

But fate had other plans for the couple. On his last trip out of town before going away for the vacation, Bendang met with an accident when his jeep fell down a deep gorge. His injuries were severe: one broken leg, a dislocated hip and a bruised face and also severe concussion. Kilang found himself attending to the husband soon after he had treated the wife. During this harrowing period, when the doctor had to deal not only with the physical injuries but also Bendang's belligerent resistance to medication and nursing, there were occasions when he feared that he might lose his patient because he seemed to have lost all will to live. He advised them to go to Vellore for further check-up and treatment where, he said, there were skilled doctors who specialized in such injuries. But Bendang would have none of it; he said if he was going to die, he would like to die in his own home and not in some strange hospital in a distant land. He had been discharged from the hospital after two weeks on his insistence and had now settled into the routine of a lethargic convalescent. Kilang found it extremely ironic that so soon after his counselling sessions with Bendang about how to handle Aosenla's post-natal depression, he was now compelled to talk to Aosenla about her husband's post-accident frame of mind. Apart from the usual check-ups and writing prescriptions, Kilang could not talk about the patient's mental problems openly with the wife within the household. Naturally, he wanted the conversation to be confidential, so he left word for her to come to his clinic the very next day if possible.

13

Aosenla too was getting increasingly worried about the drastic change in her husband; the physical injuries were extensive but he was a strong man and given time he would eventually heal. But she knew that in order to do that, he had to fight and summon the power of his will to complement the effect of the medication and nursing that he was receiving. However, it was becoming clearer by the day that Bendang was losing the will to recover and was giving in to a petulant resentment because he was now reduced to helplessness. Bendang had insisted that a male nurse be engaged who would take care of all his physical needs, saying that his wife was still weak from her own ordeal and to subject her to the exertions involved in nursing him would not be fair. So Kilang had found a person who was not only a trained nurse but also a male, and who had experience in looking after trauma patients while he was in the army. His name was Hariba, a diminutive derived from his given name Hariprasad Thapa. (His father was a Nepali ex-armyman, who had married a local girl and had become a domicile resident of the town. The diminutive was typical of the way the Aos shorten names; the first part of the name was conjoined with the male suffix ba and hence Hariba). Kilang came to know about Hariba from a colleague and persuaded him to take up the job, explaining to him what was needed of him. Another advantage was that he spoke the local language fluently besides his own mother tongue, Hindi, and also some English. He had a good physique, was always neatly dressed and did not smoke or chew paan. He was also extremely punctual and regular. But in spite of the excellent nursing he was receiving, there seemed to be very little improvement in Bendang's condition. He remained as unenthusiastic as ever about his own well-being. At times, Aosenla used to hear him abusing the nurse for any little real or imagined lapses and she was worried.

Dr Kilang's message therefore came as a happy co-incidence because she was planning to call on him to discuss the crisis at home. She went to his clinic the very day she received his invitation, telling Bendang that she was going to the market. Though she knew the general location of the clinic, she had never set foot inside the compound and the building, which housed the administrative section. Kilang was waiting on the porch when she arrived. He escorted her into his chamber and gently closed the door, indicating to his staff that they were not to be disturbed. Before Aosenla could say anything, Kilang spoke, and she was taken aback by his tone. He sounded as if he was blaming her for Bendang's state of mind. But when he saw the shock on her face, he seemed to relent and became more solicitous as he had always been with her. In a gentler tone, he asked if everything was all right in their marriage, if they had had any strong differences of opinion prior to the accident, or did they quarrel about something important after he came home from the hospital? Aosenla was not prepared for such intimate probing into their private life and was on the verge of tears, when he suddenly got up from his chair and sat next to her. She became even more surprised; what was the man doing? She wanted to get up and walk away from the man who was always so correct and courteous with her. But something curious was happening to her; she found that an irrational part of her was enjoying his physical proximity and was not allowing the prim and proper housewife in her to express her outrage. Kilang also must have sensed the odd reaction and he immediately went back to his chair and rang the bell to order some tea.

It was only after they were sipping the tea that he began to talk about Bendang and the possible changes he could make to bring him out of his present state of mind. He also prescribed new medicines, which he hoped would hasten the healing process. But, he added, that she must be prepared for further investigation in Vellore or the All India Institute of Medical Sciences in Delhi if Bendang did not show any further improvement. Aosenla sat impassive while he was talking, with a strange look on her face. Sensing that he had offended her by his earlier behaviour, Kilang started to apologize, but she cut him short and addressed him, 'Doctor, I will not pretend that ours has been a perfect marriage, but if you are implying in any way that I am neglecting him or being unmindful of his welfare then you are wrong. He is my husband and the father of my daughters. And I want to assure you that, just as you, I hold his welfare above all. I thank you for all that you have been doing and will abide by your advice on this matter. So let us keep things as they are, shall we? And I promise you, I will do my best to convince him that what you are suggesting will bring about his full recovery.' Disarming him with her usual civility and bestowing a demure smile on him, she walked out of the room to the waiting car.

Kilang was struck by the calmness with which Aosenla delivered her speech; for an instant he even thought that it was rehearsed. But how could that be? She could not have anticipated his questions, nor could she have known how he would behave with her in the privacy of his chamber. But other patients required his attention, and he left that train of thought and busied himself with their problems. Aosenla on the other hand was troubled; she thought back to the instant when he sat close to her; instead of feeling apprehensive, she had almost relished his presence. She instantly knew that she was being pulled into a dangerous territory by her physical reaction to another man and resolved that from now on she would avoid all such situations and would meet him only if a meeting became necessary for Bendang's welfare. She went home in a pensive mood and made straight for the bedroom. She had seen that Bendang was sitting in his wheel chair in the garden. She needed time to compose herself before she could face her husband and act the solicitous wife, explaining to him why she took so long. She had decided to tell him that she met Kilang quite by accident and he had insisted on her going to his clinic with him. She would tell him about the doctor's concern and then gently broach the subject of further treatment elsewhere.

She went out to where Bendang was sitting and pulled a stool, usually meant for the nurse, and sat near him and put her hand on his. He woke up with a jerk and looked at her intently. The things she saw in his eyes made her draw back her hand; she felt she was looking at an unfathomable abyss, and that the man in front of her was a total stranger. Both of them however recovered, almost at the same instant, and Bendang smiled at her sheepishly. She too returned the smile with more life in hers. Then she proceeded to spin her well-rehearsed narrative. At the end of it, she waited with some apprehension wondering what his reaction would be; would he turn his face away dismissing the idea outright, or would he utter an emphatic 'no' and stare back defiantly as he had been doing whenever the subject of outside treatment arose? To her great surprise, nothing of the sort happened; he simply gazed at her for a long time and sighed, 'Do as you and Kilang think best.' Aosenla was relieved and worried at the same time; relieved because at long last Bendang was willing to try for complete healing; worried because without Kilang's active participation in the matter, the arrangements for the trip could not be made. She had heard how difficult it was to get appointments with the specialists in these places, and that you have to have influential contacts for getting an early appointment. After the morning's encounter, she decided to withhold the news of Bendang's willingness to go for further treatment from the good doctor for some days. She needed time to restore her sense of balance in the relationship among the three of them. When Hariba came out with a cup of Bournvita for his master, Aosenla quietly withdrew into the house and went to her bedroom.

'Her' bedroom; it had literally become so ever since the nurse had been engaged. Bendang had always chafed and squirmed when his wife had to put the bedpan in place or wipe him afterwards, so one day he had insisted on hobbling to the bathroom. But the trip, attempted with the assistance of Aosenla, resulted in a clumsy fall; luckily for everyone no serious damage was done to the patient, only Aosenla scraped her shin against a stool that was standing close to door. In fact, it was this incident that initiated the search for a male attendant, and after Hariprasad joined, Bendang insisted on moving to the guest room across the corridor where an additional bed was placed for the nurse. If, in the earlier days, her bedroom was a space of conflicting experiences for Aosenla, it now became her refuge; a sanctuary where she could be free of any intrusions or painful memories of enduring the pain of her husband's drunken ardour or the memory of her own participation in torrid matings induced solely by her own fantasies of love for him. For the first time in her married life, she was experiencing a unique sense of belonging to herself, with no one or nothing compelling her to behave one way or the other. There were of course some sane moments when she tried to temper this feeling by reminding herself that the physical separation was brought about by this terrible accident to her husband and that it was purely temporary. Yet she could not help feeling that Bendang's presence in the room was gradually fading; only sometimes when his wardrobe was opened by sheer force of habit while looking for something, was she reminded of the 'crowdedness' in which they had 'lived' in this room for so many years. But today, as she lay on the huge bed, she was beset by a vague fear that another presence was impinging on her newfound freedom, a fear that had to do with a man other than her husband. She could not determine why she should have been so disturbed by the spontaneous gesture from Kilang, who might have only wanted to emphasize his concern by sitting close to her. But even as she was saying this, she knew that this rationalization was not true and that what she had been trying to articulate was the fear of her own physical reaction to his overture, and this new fear became a dark shadow lurking and threatening to cloud the sense of freedom of her mind.

When she woke up in the late afternoon from a troubled sleep, she found that everyone, including her daughters back from school, had eaten. She admonished her maid, asking her why she did not wake her up. She replied, 'Sahib asked me not to disturb you.' So she had a light meal and proceeded to help her girls with their homework. They were soon done, and happily went off to play outside. The sheer 'routineness' of it all afforded Aosenla an escape from her inner turmoil and she was happy to immerse herself in its rhythms.

Little did she imagine that a greater nightmare was about to take over her placid existence and destroy the modicum of 'normalcy' that she had been so assiduously struggling to infuse into that relationship.

14

After a light afternoon tea, as Aosenla was about to go into the pantry to see if any provisions needed to be procured, her maid came running to her breathlessly; she seemed to be in a terribly agitated state and could not speak immediately. She stood before her mistress dumb and ashen-faced. Aosenla waited for a while and eventually made her sit down and tried to calm her down. She then asked her gently, 'What's wrong? What happened?' The maid began to cry and would not say anything. Aosenla waited patiently and allowed her to sob out whatever sorrow was causing this great upheaval in her heart; she also gave her a glass of water which the girl drank gratefully, and after some time when she regained her breath, she began to speak haltingly, heartbroken sobs interfering with her speech. Looking at her mistress fearfully, the terrified girl began her story,

'Madam, I do not know how to begin; it has to do with a secret that I have long wanted to tell you about after I came to know about it. The story goes back a long time, even before you were married. But when my father learnt that I had finally landed in your home, he told me in the strongest words not to disclose this to anyone, especially you. If I disobeyed him, he said, something terrible would happen not only to me and our family but also to you. So I kept quiet all these years. But now I cannot hold the secret any more because if I do, a little girl is going to die.'

Aosenla was totally taken aback, wondering what she was trying to say and asked, 'What secret, what little girl?'

But the girl did not reply immediately; instead, she abruptly went out and looked around to see if there was anyone listening, because she remembered that she had been seen by the other servants as she had dashed off towards the main house from the back entrance, ranting and crying at the same time. When she came in, Aosenla, sensing her distress, said, 'Look, let's go and talk in a place where no one will hear us, all right? Go to your room now and wait for my call. Be sure to put on warm clothes; we are going out for a walk by the stream.'

The spot she meant was actually a little mound of earth on the edge of the property, which was close to the boundary wall. While digging the foundation for the wall, the labourers had dumped the earth in that spot and left it like that. In time, grass grew over it making it an ideal spot for relaxing outdoors. Her daughters loved this spot where they spent endless afternoons playing house-house with their dolls and kitchen things. And the stream she mentioned was not actually a natural one; it was a shallow canal-like depression along the boundary wall, and only in summer did it become one, when the abundant rain waters coursed along its length towards the lower perimeters.

Aosenla was not overly curious about the 'secret' that the girl had mentioned, but at the same time, some inner instinct told her that she should listen to what the girl had to say. She thought that it could be some gossip about the servants; or that it might have to do with the young girl's own secret. In a little while, they went out as planned and spotting a dry patch on the mound, Aosenla motioned for the girl to sit near her, and said,

'So, tell me your secret,' and waited with a smile on her face. Never even once had it occurred to Aosenla that the secret might have anything to do with her or the family; she had merely assumed that any secret in the custody of a servant would surely deal with their class and she was there merely to help the maid in her distress and help her find a solution if possible. So she was not prepared for the impact of the secret that the girl revealed to her unsuspecting self; it was so devastating that Aosenla felt as if a cruel hand was inflicting a tremendous body blow and was turning everything in her life into a chaotic mess; her very existence began to seem unreal. She felt that she was peering beyond a veil at a supposedly healthy person and discovering a rotting carcass. The abrupt beginning of the story by the frightened girl enhanced the impact because what she said was simple and stark. 'Madam,' the trembling girl began, 'sahib has another daughter, older than Chubala by some years.'

After she uttered these devastating words, the girl must have realized how the revelation would affect her mistress. She looked more frightened and began to whimper once again. It took some moments for Aosenla to grasp the import of what she had said, but when it sank in, she was too shocked to say anything. At first she did not want to believe what she had heard; but at the same time she wanted to hear the whole story. So, suppressing her anguish and with mounting dread, she somehow signalled to the storyteller to continue. The agitated girl continued: 'You see, the girl's mother was my mother's cousin, and it happened during the year that she was going to appear in her matric exams.'

Aosenla wanted to remain calm as if to distract herself from facing the truth. She calculated that the other woman would be more or less the same age as herself. Somewhat emboldened by the apparent calm on the face of her mistress, the girl continued, 'My uncle was partnering in some road construction work with sahib, and he used to come to our village quite often. When he had to spend the night in the village, he used to stay in uncle's house. That year, when my cousin was on study leave and stayed at home, he came more frequently and stayed for longer periods. My cousin fell in love with him, and even before her final exam, she became pregnant. When my uncle discovered what had happened, he confronted sahib and demanded that he marry her. People say that sahib simply laughed and walked out of the house, never to return. Uncle beat up my cousin and later sent word to sahib never to set foot in the village again. That year, uncle incurred a big loss because sahib did not pay him what he was owed. My cousin wrote her exam in March and gave birth to a daughter in October that year. My mother still remembers how the new mother refused to breast-feed the baby, and a relative with a nursing baby had to feed her. Some years after the birth of this girl, people heard that sahib was getting married to a girl from his own village.

When my uncle heard about the wedding he became very angry, and in spite of my aunt's pleas to leave things alone, uncle decided to meet sahib's father and tell him about the birth of the girl, and ask for a name from the paternal grandfather by way of acknowledging that the child was sahib's even if he was going to marry another woman. Madam, you also know that we still follow this tradition so that such unfortunate children can at least claim kinship with a clan. Uncle wanted to try and give his granddaughter at least this small status in society. Aunty was against this and pleaded with him not to be foolish. But uncle was adamant, said it was his duty to seek justice for the little girl. So he came to the town to meet the old man.'

Aosenla thought, 'It was just before our wedding, and no one would have noticed an extra villager coming to the house.'

'No one actually knows what happened; whether he met sahib or not is not clear but he certainly seemed to have met the father. When my uncle came back after a few days, he was a changed man. He told my aunty that she was right; they should forget the whole affair and not say anything more about the baby, adding that it was their daughter's fault too. Since the name of the father could not be declared officially, her clan also would remain unknown, though everyone in the village knew who had fathered this poor child. There was no name from the father's family, and so she grew up with the diminutive that her grandmother gave her, Akala, which actually is the pet term for a baby girl, any girl. Socially, uncle's family had to endure many insulting remarks because a heavy fine was imposed on my cousin for giving birth to a child out of wedlock; and not only that, but the father's name also could not be acknowledged in public.'

Aosenla's heart went out to this unknown girl who had to grow up with the stigma of a name-tag which is even worse than 'bastard'. Such children are called 'children of the streets' in Ao society, meaning 'real father not known'.

The girl continued, 'It was my aunty who suffered the most because she had to bear all the trouble of bringing up this unfortunate girl. But the villagers were surprised when very soon uncle paid off all his debts and even bought some more land to enlarge his rice paddies. Then, within a year, my youngest maternal uncle was appointed as a chowkidar in the government school of our village. Uncle also bought a cow so that the baby would have fresh milk every day. Their life seemed to have become better than before.'

After a pause, the maid started to talk again, 'My cousin continued with her studies as if nothing had happened. She was good and trained to be a nurse. Almost immediately after the results, she got a job in a tea garden in Assam and went off to live there.'

At this point Aosenla raised her hand and asked, 'What happened to your niece? Tell me about her.'

The girl calmly replied, 'I am coming to that. Let me finish the story about my aunt first. She eventually married a man from the plains and never ever came to the village even once to visit her parents. She had four children, two girls and two boys, and till now everyone talks about how hard she is because she has not allowed the children to meet the grandparents even once. It is also said that she refused to meet some of her relatives when they tried to visit her once or twice. She cut off all contact with her family.'

'Now about my niece; see, nothing is secret in the village and people talk, even of such matters, openly. So the abandoned girl came to know about her parents and how they had rejected her; the mother not breast-feeding her and the father's family not recognizing her. Perhaps she never forgave them for that; I remember how angry she was all the time, quarreling with us, her grandparents and schoolmates. She would miss classes and roam in the jungle all by herself and she became a bit wild; the grandparents did not know how to handle her. They even tried to send her to her mother once but the mother flatly refused to accept her. She took to running around with boys from an early age and last year got pregnant. But the boy, whom she named, refused to marry her saying that he was not sure whether the child she was carrying was actually his. So once again, to the great shame of our family she gave birth to a girl who can never call any man 'father'. After this rejection for the second time, the young unmarried mother suddenly took ill and died last week. The baby is only two months old. The grandparents are too old to look after her; her own grandmother, my aunt, once more refused to have anything to do with her grandchild, saying that she did not want her husband to find out the truth about her past. So, in desperation my uncle has come to town and is planning to bring the baby here to give her to you and sahib.'

As soon as Aosenla heard these words, she felt as if the sky had fallen on her head and that she was slipping into a dark hole.

As harsh and cruel as the information was to her mind, it also felt like a strong physical blow. Utterly devastated both in body and mind, she could only bow her head and sit in numbed silence for a long time. When she raised her head, it was to grab the hapless girl and shake her violently, shouting, 'If you knew all this, why did you come to work for me and why have you kept quiet about this for so many years?'

The girl did not reply immediately, only turned her face away and began to weep again. After a while she said, 'When I came to town looking for a job, I did not know anybody here as I had lived in the village all my life. It was through a friend that my aunt came to know that a family was looking for a maid and brought me to town. I stayed for a week in another auntie's house in town because my aunt could not stay away from her fields for so many days. She left me with her friend as she trusted her completely and knew that I would be placed in a good household. It was the town aunty who brought me to your house and arranged for me to work here. Back in the village, when my parents came to know where I was placed, at first they became very angry with town aunty and ordered me to come back to the village. But I refused to go back because I had grown to like you and was happy here. Town aunty was also hurt because she did not know why they were so upset and insisted that you were a good person and assured my parents that I would never suffer in your household, if that was the reason for their objection. Madam, I swear that I did not know anything about what I am telling you now. It was only after some years with you when I went to the village during a Christmas holiday that I came to know about my cousin and her liaison with sahib. That was when I understood why my parents were angry with town aunty and had asked me to leave this job earlier. Town aunty did not know anything then; but since grandfather is staying with them, I do not know if he has told her the history of the baby.'

She took a deep breath and continued, 'That time too they told me not to stay back but I had grown to love you because you were good to me and I had become very fond of the girls. Besides, after living with you here, I can never live in the village again. When they saw that I was determined to come back here, they made me promise that I would not say a word about what happened in the past to anybody; otherwise, my father swore, there would be dire consequences. So I kept my promise, hoping that you would never find out.'

The maid must have sensed how much her story was hurting her mistress and another bout of sobbing overtook her. But she got a hold on herself and went on; 'Today as I was feeding the chickens, someone came to the back gate and told me about uncle's visit. Learning that he was going to bring the baby to the house, I got scared and so I decided to tell you the truth. Please forgive me madam for having to bring this terrible news to you.'

The girl was sobbing again as she concluded her story and in a tearful voice added, 'Madam please do something to save the baby; the man said that she is crying non-stop and that sometimes she cannot breathe properly on account of this.' She knelt before her mistress, begging her to save the little girl's life.

The shock of learning so much painful history in this manner was too much for Aosenla and she was fuming with an inner rage. But there was an inexplicable softening immediately afterwards and she too began to sob when she thought of the unknown baby's miserable plight. When the anger and grief abated somewhat, she realized that something had to be done immediately to contain the ramifications of this ugly truth from her husband's past. Feeling extremely angry at this betrayal, her first impulse was to shout, 'Very good, let all the world see what kind of a family this is.' But within the turmoil in her heart, Aosenla found that an inner force was compelling her maternal instincts to come to the fore, subsuming her personal anger and hatred for the moment. It became clear to her, from the maid's extreme concern, that the baby was indeed in a precarious condition and needed immediate medical attention. She knew that she had to act fast if the impending disaster was to be averted. So she decided to take care of the baby's problem first. Once again, wondering where to turn for help, she could think only of Kilang, who would not only help her out but would also be discreet.

15

The moment she took the decision, she became a different person. She got up abruptly and instructed the exhausted maid to go look for the doctor and ask him to come to the house immediately. Only after that was she to go looking for her uncle, and request him to stay wherever he was and say nothing to anybody until madam or the doctor contacted him. She then went towards the house dreading the prospect of meeting Bendang, but luckily for her when she went inside, she learnt that he was feeling a bit tired and had gone off to sleep. It was a momentary reprieve for her; she hastily freshened up, got into a clean dress and asked for a cup of tea. Only then did she feel a bit normal and waited impatiently for Kilang to appear. As it turned out, he had been about to go home when the frantic maid delivered the message, therefore he had come straight to the house. He wanted to know what had happened, why the urgency, was Bendang worse, or was anyone else hurt? To all these questions, Aosenla answered with a finger to her lips and asked him to accompany her to a room at the end of the corridor, which was used as Bendang's office. It was at some distance from where Bendang was now lodged. She closed the door hurriedly, and in a somewhat dispassionate and jumbled manner told him what she had learnt on that calamitous day. She came straight to the point and asked if he could take another stray into his orphanage. Kilang was taken by surprise, as much by the order of her priorities as by the force of the desperate plea in her voice. He also noted how close she was to breaking down; there was no time for him to probe and argue, though a nagging voice at the back of his mind was cautioning him against any hasty decision. Sensing the slight reluctance in his manner, Aosenla pulled him by the hand and said, 'We have no time to lose, I'll send my maid with you to the house where the baby is crying her lungs out and you take her to your orphanage right away. All other formalities and money matters, I'll settle with you soon. And please, not a word to Bendang, I'll handle that too.' Opening the door silently, she pushed him out saying, 'Go, the girl is waiting for you by the gate.' And in a minute Kilang drove out of the compound with the maid, leaving all the secret tangles for Aosenla to unscramble and set right, if humanly possible. As though scripted by an unseen hand, the priorities for Aosenla changed irrevocably; Bendang and his physical problems became redundant in the face of a tremendous truth manifested in the birth of a little girl into a cruel world. The little girl's mother would be barely in her teens, just a year or two older than her own daughter Chubala. And Aosenla felt a chill in her heart thinking, what if...But she quickly banished the dark thoughts and began to concentrate on what more needed to be done in order to ward off the disaster, which threatened to destroy her family.

None of the players in the fate-ordained drama realized until much later the impact of this extraordinary turn of events on their lives. They were still unaware of how the equations in their lives had changed forever the instant the doctor persuaded the great-grandfather to give up the child. The old man was initially suspicious and was not willing to part with the baby, insisting that he would give her only to Bendang and his family. So the doctor took them both to his Home and finally convinced the old man that she would be safe and that her rehabilitation would start immediately. He called for the old Matron and asked her to clean up the baby, dress her in new clothes and after feeding her, bring her back to the old man sitting in the doctor's office. While his order was being carried out, Kilang began to reason with the old man, saying that he should think only of the baby's welfare and not create problems for Bendang's family over a matter in which he too had played a role. The time to raise the points of justice for his daughter was over, and he had let it pass for whatever reasons that had dictated his actions then. Kilang pointed out that apart from creating a scandal, he would gain nothing; on the other hand if he insisted on doing what he planned, he would be responsible for his great-granddaughter's death too. Was he prepared to bear the responsibility, Kilang asked. Just as he finished saying this, as if on cue, the freshly bathed baby in new clothes was brought to the two men. She was now sleeping quietly and looked serene. After a while, she was taken back to her crib.

When the great-grandfather saw the transformation in the baby, he broke down; holding the doctor's hand, and amidst heaving sobs, began to speak in a small voice, almost inaudible, so Kilang had to lean closer in order to hear what he was saying.

'Doctor,' he said haltingly, 'we had heard about your Home and wondered what kind of crazy man you were, going around picking up other people's abandoned children, feeding them and looking after them. We had asked, what for? I still don't understand why you do this; but I am happy that you do because now I know that this child will have the future that I could not give her mother. From now on, she is yours, I give you my word.' He handed in the signed form and went out of the room without another word. Kilang's driver took him back to his lodgings and Kilang never heard from him again. As the good doctor went in to the nursery to check on the latest entrant, he knew that something momentous had happened to his orderly life the moment he accepted the piece of paper with the old man's signature.

By drawing Kilang into the vortex of this family drama, Aosenla made him not only an accomplice to the fact, but also an exclusive party in sharing the knowledge of this secret. Bendang had somehow remained at the periphery of the intuitive link between Aosenla and Kilang; although his condition had so far largely determined the public performance of the two, especially Aosenla's. Bendang had always occupied centre stage but now Aosenla and Kilang were privy to the dark secret of his youth, which had the potential of knocking him offstage altogether. They also had the huge responsibility of circumventing the ramifications of this truth if the status quo was to be maintained.

Bendang did not know that while he slept the disturbed sleep of the maimed, his world had taken a tumble and that he was now facing the inevitable dénouement, should the dark truth of his past be exposed. The ace in this game of fortune was held by Aosenla and no one, including she, knew at this juncture what she would do with it. Whereas up until now, it was she who had always remained in the shadow of her husband and his needs, she now had become the main player, though it would take quite some time for her to either recognize or accept this role. Only one role seemed to have remained static: that of Kilang as the mediator, Kilang as the pacifier and facilitator. But the moment he persuaded the old man to leave the baby in his Home, he had, willy-nilly become an accomplice in this game. He also gradually recognized the fact that he was now inextricably linked to the fate of this family, which would be eventually determined by Aosenla. He had acted on her wishes because there was no time for questions or protests. Afterwards, when he mulled over the extraordinary events of that evening, he neither felt anger nor resentment at having to respond to her call for help and thus getting entangled in the web. He had to admit that the plight of the baby and the ethics of his profession had compelled him to do what was best for the child at that crucial moment. He also felt that there was an inevitability to everything that had happened that night.

What had primarily motivated Bendang to engage the male nurse and remove himself from the master bedroom, and in the process from Aosenla's constant presence and supervision, was his desire to feel independent, physically and mentally, just as he was during the pre-accident days. That he would still need the nurse's assistance did not bother him, because he was an outsider and a male and was experienced in dealing with injuries sustained in combat or accident. He also knew that the relationship would be totally impersonal and he need not feel any shame or awkwardness on account of his present state of helplessness. While still in his old room, he felt that his physical disability had been eroding his self-esteem and he did not want to feel dependent on his wife, because even to do a simple thing like getting into or out of the bed, he needed her assistance. And then there was the matter of disposing bodily waste; how he hated it when the two of them had to jostle and push and pull the vessel to put it in the right position. This situation was becoming intolerable and Bendang had turned to Kilang for help. That is how the male nurse came to live in the house, and Bendang moved out of the bedroom and away from these mortifying and even humiliating moments under his wife's constant supervision. The new arrangement thus afforded him an enormous sense of freedom and now that he did not need her physical attention any more, he was content to know that she was there somewhere in the house as she always had been.

Early in the evening, when Bendang woke from his restful nap, he was told that Dr Kilang had dropped by, but when he was told that sahib was sleeping, he'd left. Bendang did not say anything; he merely nodded. When Aosenla came in, he was struck by her altered appearance and asked her why she was looking so tired; she replied that she had a severe headache and that she had come to tell him that she would retire early. Tonight of all nights, she dreaded the prospect of sitting at the table with him at dinner and luckily for her, the headache would save her the ordeal of maintaining the pretended civility in front of the girls and servants. She retired to her room where she was joined by her daughters. They chatted with their mother about their school and friends. But they could see that their mother was distracted, so they trooped out after only a short while and went into their father's room where he had ordered dinner for the three of them. Aosenla had declined dinner and asked the maid to bring her only a bowl of soup and an apple. This would also afford her some private moments with the girl. When she entered the room carrying a tray, Aosenla asked her to shut the door and sit by her bed. Then, in a calm voice, she began to talk to the maid who had not yet recovered from the events of the day. Aosenla assured her that the baby would be well looked after in the doctor's Home; but she was never to try to visit her or talk about her to anybody. In order to retain her control over the girl, she added that she was still very hurt and angry that she had withheld the truth from her mistress from whom she had received only kindness and love all these years. That act alone proved that she had not been honest with her benefactor. And now if anything she said or did put the family in any kind of danger, Aosenla added that she would be implicated and who knew even the police might interrogate her about the orphan girl. The mention of police turned out to be a real deterrent; the maid was visibly shaken and readily gave her word to her mistress, adding how sorry she was for not saying anything about their family's secret earlier. Dismissing the still-troubled maid, Aosenla finished her soup and absent-mindedly began to munch on the apple thinking, 'one loose end tied up'.

16

As soon as this thought crossed her mind, Aosenla sat up in surprise: why was she thinking this way? Wasn't she outraged at all? Didn't she feel betrayed? Didn't she want to confront Bendang with this truth? For a long time she remained awake, tossing and turning on the enormous bed, beset by many conflicting thoughts. Ever since Bendang had moved to the guest room, she'd begun to feel quite free, but tonight as she lay curled up in a corner of the big bed, the quietness seemed only to enlarge his absence. Why was this happening? She told herself that she was not missing her husband, the man; it was rather like missing the idea of a husband on the conjugal bed. But she found the absolute silence in the room unnerving, as though an emptiness had been created and she alone could not fill that space. In the face of the shocking revelations and hectic exertions of the evening, this was a totally contrary sensation for her and she could not understand why it should be so. Had the years of living together as husband and wife put such a stamp on her psyche that she subconsciously sought his presence during a crisis? Ironic, because she had not shared a close companionship with him, but over the years, a sort of unarticulated sense of 'togetherness' had developed, because of which perhaps the marriage had survived and retained a façade of normalcy. As she mulled over the day's revelations and dreaded what tomorrow would bring, she immediately understood that she had needed someone to talk to. But if she had longed, during that fleeting moment, to have another person in the room, she realized that it should never have been Bendang, because he was the villain in the drama. Why then had she felt his absence?

She understood, even though she could not say it in so many words, that this sense of togetherness was habit-forming. For her, having her husband by her side always had become a norm and she derived a sense of security from that togetherness. What she had learnt during the course of that evening was a truth that she could not handle alone; she needed someone, a trusted friend or relative to put that knowledge in perspective before she decided on a course of action. And Bendang was not that person, because he was the perpetrator of the crime in the first place. Yet, for some fleeting moments, she had longed for his companionship. She thought of her mother then; but instantly realized that she would only tell her to let bygones be bygones. She then remembered how difficult it was to talk to her mother about even the simplest thing. She would have to retreat strategically before answering her questions or reacting to her remarks, obviously for fear of incurring the displeasure of her husband if her responses were contrary to his views. She had herself lived on that principle when her father was alive and continued to do so with her brothers and their wives. Ruefully she thought, if there was a living martyr, it was her mother. She also knew that she could never confide in her brothers or sisters-in-law because they too had maintained an attitude of civil distance from Bendang and his family. The tragedy of her life, she thought, was that there was really no one with whom she could share moments of anguish or of happiness.

Turning and tossing on the huge bed, she tried to concentrate on the account given by her maid, and for the briefest of moments wondered whether it could be a fabrication of some sort. But the more she thought about it, the more convinced she became of the veracity of the story. According to her reasoning, simple village people did not go about fabricating stories like this when it touched people of substance like her in-laws. She also ruled out any form of blackmail and surmised that the old man was simply tired of carrying the burden of his youthful greed, now so hideously grown into an enormous guilt with the birth of this unwanted baby girl. He desperately wanted to divest himself of the responsibility and had come here to return that which belonged to this family. They had the wherewithal whereas he was only an accomplice of the dark past and did not want the blood of this innocent baby also on his hands. What the old man had done was out of sheer desperation, a step undertaken as a last resort in order to save this child who was as much his flesh and blood as she was theirs. He did not seek anything in return, maybe only absolution for his past actions by helping save this child born to such grief. But the solution to the present predicament was not as easy as he thought because he knew that the existence of this baby now touched on the future of this influential family.

Aosenla felt a physical constriction in her body that threatened to choke the life-force out of her, and with an effort she sat up on the bed, looking wildly around her. The earlier shock had somehow been absorbed by the frantic activities that had followed. But now, she was beginning to feel that another onslaught of shock was imminent. What should she do with the truth? What would confronting Bendang achieve? Would her life be the same? Was she prepared to give up the life she had been nurturing by exposing this dark secret? What about the future of her daughters? What would be the consequence of a direct confrontation? These and such other questions assailed her and she felt that she was being sucked into a quagmire of doubts. But all the while an inner voice urged her to stay calm and patient. She had to dredge up her last mental resources to regain some composure, and she sat on the bed breathing deeply of the night air.

With an effort, she went to the bathroom and washed her face. She rummaged in the medicine cabinet for something to soothe her nerves. Surely, she hoped, not all the medicines prescribed for Bendang had been transferred to the other room? After the first frantic moments, she found a small bottle with some sleeping pills tucked away in a corner of the cabinet. She threw them on to her palm and counted; there were nine of them. Her first desperate impulse was to gulp them all down; but something held her back. The crazed moment passed, and she looked at the promise contained in the tiny pills dispassionately. She touched them in a sort of meditative contemplation, and in the end, took only two with a glass of water and returned the rest to the bottle, pushing it back to its original resting place. Almost in a daze she stumbled back to the bed and tried to sleep.

But her mind was in such a state that she tossed and turned for a long time. Eventually however, the pills did their work and she fell asleep in the wee hours of the morning. When she awoke, her head was clear. Her first thoughts were of the baby and the immediate sensation was one of relief in knowing that at least for the time being, she was alive and in safe hands. As she prepared to come out of her room and face the rest of the household, there was no sign of the agitated woman of the night before. In the calmness of the morning, she knew that she had to keep her wits about her in such a volatile situation. However painful and ugly this knowledge was, she resolved not to allow it to overwhelm her reason and patience, because what she did now would not only drastically alter the course of her life but also make or mar her daughters' future. The entire burden of the family had fallen upon her since Bendang's accident and now coping with the new knowledge had become an additional responsibility. It was apparent that Aosenla was stepping into yet another level of consciousness, a consciousness of practical reality.

If in the past, she had dealt with reality in a more subjective way, now she found herself deliberately subsuming the self and re-balancing her perception about the present situation. Once she accepted this idea, she began to view her predicament more objectively and focused on fixing things so that the even tenor of her life did not change in any visible way. Though the past seemed to have caught up with Bendang's present, she realized that she had to somehow beat back this tide. The enterprise had to begin from the present moment and Aosenla had to sort out her priorities and go about taking care of them in a calculated way, so that the façade of normalcy and everyday calm was maintained.

Now that the baby was taken care of, even if temporarily, Aosenla decided to set aside her personal grievances and concentrate on the needs of her family. It was difficult; she was demanding a great sacrifice from herself. How could any woman remain so calm after learning of the perfidy of the man she called husband? He had married her under false pretences. Not only that, she could not imagine how this family, who always pretended to be so prim and proper, had such an abominable blot on their history. But she immediately realized that recriminations of this sort would lead only to more chaos and that she had to take control of her emotions if she were to succeed in her scheme of saving the future for her daughters. She was acutely aware that she was contemplating a sort of deceit, just as Bendang and his family had maintained all these years. But, she quickly rationalized that her lie was going to be for the benefit of all concerned, including the unfortunate child now in Kilang's Home. However tenuous the justification was, it helped her to re-focus on her priorities in order to put the new charade in motion. Though she told herself she was doing this for her daughters' future and to protect them from their father's infamy, inwardly Aosenla was beginning to feel a vicarious sense of triumph in being privy to this dark truth. She somehow felt that she now had the upper hand in their relationship, which had always been about Bendang's needs and whims. His image in her mind was certainly diminished and Aosenla felt that he was not so overwhelming after all. This conviction gave her a lot of relief.

17

In this new situation, Aosenla decided that the first priority had to be her husband's rehabilitation, a process that had been under consideration before all this happened. Since Bendang had expressed his willingness to go to a bigger hospital for treatment, she decided to pursue this by enlisting Kilang's help. It would also be an excellent opportunity for her to find out about the baby. But first, Kilang had to be informed that Bendang was now willing to undertake the journey. So he was requested to come to the house in the evening so that the doctor could hear it from the patient himself.

Kilang was surprised to receive the message: what was Aosenla planning now? He was also worried, wondering if the woman was going to tell her husband about the events of the previous day in his presence, making him a party to the dark drama that was threatening to engulf this family. And if his direct complicity in the baby's entry to his Home became known to Bendang, how would he react? He had expected that Aosenla would come first thing in the morning to enquire about the baby; but she did not. Later in the day, he received the request to come to the house. He spent an uneasy day in the hospital and came to the Home after lunch. He found the baby was responding well to the changed environment; she had adapted to bottle-feeding and all her vital signs were satisfactory. But under his seemingly calm exterior, Kilang too was under great emotional stress. He did not want any further involvement with this family beyond the care of Bendang and would have liked to stay as far away from Aosenla as possible.

Of late, he was beginning to sense that she distracted him from himself and the structured life he had made with his gentle wife and two children. He was following a profession, which he had admired since childhood, and to add to his happiness, his Home gave him a lot of satisfaction. He was admired and respected by the town; the local church often spoke of his 'sacrifice' as a glowing example of selfless love for humanity. He had a stature in society and his image as an exemplary citizen and family man was well established. But in spite of such public adulation, Kilang had remained a humble man, always down-to-earth and ready to help a needy or sick person without expecting anything in return. The only thing he lacked was ready cash for the Home, but somehow, he always managed to meet the expenses of his establishment and sometimes, to his great amazement, funds would arrive in the nick of time from unexpected sources. One particular instance always reminded him of the saying, 'God works in mysterious ways'. A big consignment of medicines and nutritional food packets had arrived and was lying in the Post Office for payment and delivery. Kilang was stone-broke and if he did not redeem it within the deadline, which was two days away, the consignment would be returned to the sender and he would lose a valuable supply source. The good doctor was facing the biggest financial crisis of his career as the Supervisor of the Home because this very firm had many times before come to his aid by supplying goods at very reasonable prices. And if he failed to keep his end of the bargain, he might lose their goodwill and service forever. It would be a disaster because only this firm could supply the best quality medicines and the best food products for the children in the Home.

He was sitting dejectedly in his office on the penultimate day of the deadline, when there was a loud knock at his door, and immediately someone barged into his room shouting, 'Where is the good Samaritan?' It turned out that the loud voice belonged to an old classmate who had made good in the business world and had become a multi-millionaire. He lived in Kolkata, and had come home to visit his parents. When he heard that his friend, the timid Kilang, had become somewhat of a small-town celebrity, he decided to pay him a visit and so there he was. And without much preamble, this friend, with the confidence of the rich, loudly announced that when he heard of the Home and that his very dear friend Kilang was running it, he had come there himself to offer a modest donation. Fumbling in his coat pocket, he brought out a fat envelope and pushed it towards the doctor. The abruptness of the gesture took Kilang by surprise, but he remained calm and asked in a small voice, 'What is this?' His friend laughed and answered, 'A small token of my pride in our friendship, use it for the Home.' After some banter and tea, the friend left and drove off in his brand new car. Closing the door after him, Kilang touched the envelope gingerly and looked inside; there were five bundles of hundred rupee notes, the bank wrappings and staples still intact in each. Fifty thousand rupees, out of the blue and just when he needed the money most! Kilang was not an overtly religious person but that morning he went down on his knees and thanked God for this miraculous deliverance.

Unexpected windfalls like this bolstered Kilang's faith in what he was doing and the growing recognition of his services gave him a certain status in society. He valued it and had always made a conscious effort to maintain that image in all that he said and did in public. The recent unease he felt in Aosenla's presence threatened to upset this equilibrium and inwardly he resented it. But he could not ignore the present summons; it would be out of form to do so and so he went. On his way to Bendang's house, Kilang began to worry about the reason for the meeting: had Aosenla confronted her husband with the recent revelations? What should he say if it was found out that the baby was in his Home? How would Bendang react? But deep in his mind he was thinking that Aosenla was too shrewd a woman to fritter away this clout over her husband with just the three of them present, and that calmed him down a bit. When he reached the house, he was escorted straight to the drawing room where he found both husband and wife sitting in amiable silence. Aosenla stood up and shook his hand in greeting and Kilang went to Bendang and took both his hands in his. The earlier misgivings in Kilang's mind were momentarily set aside as he too settled down in one of the chairs. For a short moment, all three of them remained silent; it was finally Bendang who cleared his throat and introduced the subject of his treatment. He at first thanked Kilang for his devoted attendance on him and added; 'Kilang, you have been advising me to go for further examinations in a bigger hospital and each time I have rejected the suggestion. But I have now come to realize how sound your advice was and how foolish I have been to disregard it. Now I am ready; so why don't you two work out the details? I want to start the new treatment as soon as possible.'

He fell silent after delivering this almost rehearsed speech and looked at his wife like a child seeking appreciation after a performance. Kilang was amazed; how had Aosenla managed to convince this hard man so fast? He of course had no idea that this was accomplished before the nightmare of the previous evening. He maintained his composure and replied with a smile, 'Bendang, this is the best news that I have heard in a long while, and of course I will call up my friends in both places and see which would suit your needs most. It may take few days but I will keep you informed.' As an afterthought, he added while sipping tea, 'By the way, if it becomes difficult for me to come here, may I request madam to drop by in the Home when I send word?' It sounded like an innocuous query and yet Kilang was surprised by his own words. Why did he say that? Aosenla too was taken aback, wondering if he knew about Bendang's earlier reluctance to allow his wife to involve herself with the Home. Bendang too was thinking; did Aosenla tell the doctor about their first conversation regarding the Home? But almost at the same instant, all three of them managed to recover their composure and the air of cordiality was restored. Bendang replied in exaggerated cheerfulness, 'Why of course, it won't be a problem, will it, Asen?' She replied to this with genuine relief, 'Not at all, in fact I'd love to see your Home doctor, I've heard so much about it and have always wanted to see it for myself.'

Afterwards, Kilang thought that he need not have worried about the meeting and was glad that he could help Bendang in finding a satisfactory course of treatment and hopefully, eventual recovery. But worries of a different nature came back; what was Aosenla's game? What was she planning for the baby? Why hadn't she contacted him? He simply could not figure out this woman. When he woke up in the morning, his first thoughts were for the baby and he was certain that he would hear from Aosenla during the day enquiring about the child. Instead, there came a message about the meeting which had just concluded. There was a dangerous moment during the discussion when he had blurted out the question about her visiting the Home. He still could not understand why he had done so. But now that it was done, he thought maybe, he wanted her to come and tell him what to do about the baby, that's all; there was nothing personal in it. Still troubled, he drove home thinking. 'Will I ever be free of involvement with this family?' But he had to admit that the doctor-patient relationship, which started on such a professional note when he took up Aosenla's case, had now evolved into something more personal after Bendang's accident. And now another more important, and at the same time dangerous, element bound him inextricably to the affairs of this family. For the present however, he had committed himself by suggesting the further treatment, so from the very next day he started making phone calls to both Delhi and Vellore whenever possible or sending telegrams to various people in both places asking for information and advice.

18

In the meantime, during dinner that evening, Bendang told the girls what they had discussed with the doctor and said, 'Listen girls, I have something to tell you. As soon as uncle Kilang finalizes the arrangements, mummy and I will travel either to Vellore or New Delhi for daddy's treatment.'

Hearing this Narola piped up, 'What about Oya and me? Who will look after us?'

At this, the father smiled and replied, 'You are big girls now, and you can look after yourselves. Besides, Onula is there and grandfather Obu and grandmother Otsu are also there to look after you.'

The elder sister Chubala gave her sister an admonishing look, and said, 'Oh Naro, don't talk like a baby, don't you want daddy to become all right like before?'

Then looking at her parents, she said, 'Mummy, daddy, don't worry about us. I am there to keep an eye on Naro and will make sure that she does her homework and wears her shoes right.'

At this, all of them burst out laughing because Narola had a habit of wearing her shoes on the wrong feet and claiming that the shoes had worn out and she needed a new pair! Aosenla was touched by her elder daughter's protective attitude towards the younger and thought how quickly a girl develops these motherly instincts. That night, all four of them went to bed with their separate thoughts about the future.

Back in her bed, Aosenla tried to banish all thoughts about the future or the present, and to fall asleep with the sense of happiness she had experienced during dinner. But try as she might, the spectre of the baby girl sleeping in her crib in the Home kept on intruding. Once the baby's safety was ensured, she wanted to postpone seeing her as long as possible. Bendang's consent only a day before all this happened was fortuitous, and therefore she had initiated the meeting with Kilang as a logical follow-up action. She did this also because she wanted to divert her mind from the implications of the baby's very existence and her complicity in bringing her to Kilang's Home. She wanted to keep this issue as far away as possible from the affairs of her home. She also knew how dangerous it was to take up this 'case' when her emotions were still fraught with so much anger and resentment. Above all, she had always considered Bendang's medical treatment as her primary duty as his wife and the mother of his children. Moreover, it was an ongoing process that needed to be concluded one way or the other. But during the next few days, it was all she could do to hold herself back from visiting the Home in order to see the baby.

After about ten days, Kilang sent word that he wanted to pay them a visit to finalize the travel plans. But when he reached their house, he was surprised to find Bendang's parents sitting in the living room. After the obligatory greetings, Kilang opened the discussion by saying that he had spoken to his friends in the two hospitals and that it was for Bendang to decide where to go. But before Bendang could say anything, his father spoke up and said that he wanted Bendang to go to Vellore because it was a Christian hospital. No one said anything after this and it became obvious to Kilang that the father's wish was the final word. Then came the question of who would accompany Bendang; here again, the father said that the male nurse would of course have to go with him and then added that he had asked his eldest son-in-law to accompany them because custom demanded that such services be rendered by sons-in-law. Aosenla looked at her husband, in order to remind him of their earlier discussion and hoped that he would insist on taking her as well but he remained mute. So there was no other discussion, no small talk either; only the dates to be settled and Kilang was told that he would be informed as soon as the train tickets were purchased so that he could inform his doctor friends in Vellore.

Kilang was a reasonable man and was not easily provoked. But this evening he was truly irritated because he was made to feel like a mere errand boy. And what's more, he was disappointed to see both Bendang and Aosenla so opinionless in the presence of the parents and felt resentful that he too had been pushed into that peripheral circle. He had expected to be consulted about Bendang's health and about the relative merits of the facilities in the two places, but those details never came up for consideration. Vellore won out because it was a Christian hospital. It was also apparent that the decision had already been taken before his arrival and he need not have come at all; after all he was only told to make some more phone calls. He felt particularly slighted by the manner in which the old man conducted the whole meeting, without once asking him about Bendang's prognosis. He wondered how the old man behaved with his other children – who held important government offices - and whether he interfered with their family affairs in the same way. From his demeanour, Kilang could see that Bendang's father truly belonged to another era. His resentment notwithstanding, he admitted that had he been in a similar situation, he also might have succumbed to the pressures of old parents. He felt a bit sorry for Bendang and Aosenla. That night, Kilang went home in a reflective mood thinking about the amount of pressure that tradition could still exert upon a seemingly modern generation.

Aosenla was overcome by a tearing rage; everything seemed to have gone contrary to her plans. She had so wanted to accompany her husband when he undertook this journey. She felt that Bendang would have liked it because prior to the meeting, they had discussed this with a lot of enthusiasm and agreed that she should be there to take care of things like filling up prescriptions, making payments and seeing to other arrangements. Incidentally, they too had opted for Vellore because they were told that they could rent rooms very close to the hospital where attendants were looked after by honest guides. Moreover, they also wanted to explore the possibility of sending their older daughter Chubala to study medicine at Vellore. Now the old man had spoken and though the destination was still Vellore, Aosenla would have nothing to do with the journey, and exploration of that institute as a prospect for Chubala had to be deferred.

She could not decide with whom she was angrier; her husband or his father, for allowing such a situation to develop. Aosenla had thought, given how enthusiastic Bendang had been, that her husband was a more assertive person now and that he would be able to set aside the father's interference in their plans. But she was mistaken; Bendang had not been able to assert himself at all. The brother-in-law, Aosenla admitted, was a good soul, but she also knew that he would be lost in an unfamiliar city and instead of being a help he would be more of a liability. The father was looking at the journey more from the customary correctness of form rather than any real concern for Bendang's medical needs. And if the son wanted to submit to his father's will all his life that was his problem. But she promised herself that she would not allow that to happen to her plans for the girls. The grandparents were already hinting that Chubala would be eminently suitable for a career in the church because she was so gentle and caring. Aosenla resented this interference in her daughter's future because the girl had already chosen her career. She wanted to be a medical doctor and had made her mother promise her that she would convince the father to let her take up this profession. From the evening's experience, Aosenla doubted if she could depend on Bendang's firm support on this matter if it came to a contest with the old man's will. But for her the evening's verdict on Vellore only made her more determined to fight for her daughter's wish when the time came.

Bendang too was in a foul mood; as always, his father had upstaged him and managed to make him look like a complete wimp in public. What cut him up most was the fact that Kilang witnessed his complete capitulation to his father's autocratic ways and how small he had felt in the presence of a peer. He seethed inside for having made such a sorry spectacle of himself and was full of dark thoughts against the old man. He did not bother about the fact that Aosenla knew what the old man was like. After all, they were married now for more than fifteen years and had suffered his interference time and again. But it galled him no end that he was exposed before an outsider, and that too the doctor who was treating him. He felt like hitting out at the man who had always made him feel small because he was the only one in the family who had not graduated from college and did not hold a government office. He thought bitterly that when his father had needed a partner to start a business after retiring from service, he had pointed out to Bendang his pathetic record in studies, and somehow managed to entice him to join him in contract work, saying that he could soon be a rich man. That the father-son duo did make a lot of money in their ventures seemed to recede into the background as he mulled over the fiasco of the evening. Bendang now asked, 'What good is the money? Even to go for my own medical treatment I have to toe his line. Very well, if he thinks he can still ride roughshod over my needs and feelings, I'll not go anywhere if I cannot take my wife with me.' He was already blaming himself for letting her down by not reasoning with his father during the meeting. Why did he not say that they had already made plans and that she would go with him? As his nurse settled him in bed, he made a mental note that first thing in the morning he would tell his father that he did not want to travel anywhere yet. Instead, he would stay at home and start the physiotherapy course, which he had been postponing for months. Even in this indirect opposition, he would not be able to state the real reason for his abrupt change of heart, and he felt even more miserable, realizing how his father's domineering attitude had always prevented him from taking important decisions for himself, and had made him into such a coward.

None of the private thoughts of these three people eventually mattered, because in the middle of the night, the old man suffered a stroke and had to be rushed to the only hospital in town. But like all government hospitals, the essential equipment necessary for such an emergency was not available there. So after rudimentary first-aid measures, the patient was transferred to the army hospital, thanks to Bendang's army cronies, and admitted in the Intensive Care Unit, where he appeared to be responding to the medical procedures. But he suffered another massive stroke and slipped into a coma. He remained comatose for more than a week and early on a Sunday morning he breathed his last.

The funeral, which was held the next day, was an event in itself; all the big names of the town and the neighbouring areas turned up to pay their last respects to a man who had directly or indirectly helped develop the small township into an influential seat of power in the region. For the family, they felt not only bereft but truly orphaned, because his towering presence had dominated all their lives by guiding, cajoling and more often than not by manoeuvring their lives with an aim to place the family in the highest echelons of the emerging elite class of the town. Of all the siblings, it was Bendang who felt the most helpless. While his brothers and sisters had the cushion of secure jobs in high places, it was he alone who had depended so much on his father's strength to see him through numerous crises in his life.

As Bendang sat brooding, his thoughts went back to his youthful fling with the simple village girl whom he had impregnated. Had it not been his father's adept handling of the girl's father, he would most probably have been forced to marry her or at least to acknowledge paternity and would have been paying child support. He would surely have become a laughing stock among his town cronies and would have remained forever the family's black sheep. But nothing of the sort happened because as always, his father had managed the crisis smoothly. He never found out how exactly his father took care of the affair but not a whiff of scandal touched the family. He had then taken up with a smart educated girl of his village who was only too willing to be wooed by a member of this influential family and was slowly working her way towards the altar. The father kept a close watch on the ongoing affair; when he decided that this match was unsuitable for his designs, he pulled in the reins on his son's romantic dalliance with the unfortunate girl. He called his son into his study and they had a long talk; even the mother was kept out of the discussion. When Bendang emerged from his father's study, he looked subdued and crestfallen. At dinner that night the father announced to the family that Bendang had agreed that a proposal be sent to this obscure girl's family and that he was confident it would be accepted. Shortly after, the hurriedly arranged marriage with Aosenla took place as planned and here he was now, a respected member of the business community with a wife who had also lately become quite a personality on her own merits. Coping with the consequences of his father's sudden death became, for Bendang, much more important than his accident and the present state of his body. He thought that to go on the planned trip at this juncture would not be right. He resolved that he would have to overcome his physical problems so that he could take over his father's place in the affairs of the family. He reasoned that while all his siblings were within the bonds of rules and regulations, he alone was free from these encumbrances. This was a moment to savour; to step into the shoes of the one who had always towered over everyone in the family. Just thinking about this made him feel better and he could not wait for the mourning period to be over so that he could assume this new role and prove to one and all, especially Aosenla, that he too was a leader.

19

When Bendang told Aosenla that he was going to postpone the trip, she did not say anything because she had sensed that her husband was unhappy with the manner in which the old man had scuttled his plans. This turn of events, however, posed a problem for her. Earlier when it had become apparent that she was not going to travel with her husband, she'd been relieved; his absence would provide her with the perfect opportunity to settle the matter of the little girl. But Bendang's presence once again brought on the sense of helplessness and along with it came the old fear. But she did not have much time to brood. After the mourning period was over, the families of the siblings dispersed, and her mother-in-law became her sole responsibility. The old lady had visibly aged in the short time after her husband's death. For the first time since she'd been in the family, Aosenla saw the formidable matriarch looking absolutely lost. She seemed a shadow of her former self as she kept muttering to herself, 'A widow, I am a widow, how will I survive?' Then she would break into sobs and another soliloquy would follow, 'I always prayed to God to let me go first, but He did not listen to my prayers. What will I do now?' Aosenla felt sorry for the old woman and did everything in her power to comfort her. She took over the management of the big house, making the lethargic servants clean the house and compounds from top to bottom. She got rid of a lot of unnecessary things which she distributed to the servants, making them happy. She personally supervised the old woman's baths, making her wear decent clothes; she cooked delicious soups when she refused to touch any solid food. But when a particular soup dish was brought to her, she would look at it intently and burst out, 'It was his favourite soup, how can I eat it alone?' and sweep it off the table. Aosenla understood that along with the grief over his death, it was the old woman's absolute dependence on her husband which had made her so utterly helpless at his passing away.

When her efforts to soothe and reason with her mother-in-law failed, Aosenla turned to her husband for advice, and almost casually he asked her to call Kilang as if this doctor could provide solutions to all the problems of the family. As an afterthought, he added, 'And when he comes, I'll tell him about the postponement myself. I'll also ask him to call the physiotherapist from Jorhat here to start my course.' At this, Aosenla perked up, thinking: is this person the petulant, lethargic Bendang of just two weeks ago? But it was just a passing thought and without a murmur she sent word to Kilang, requesting him to visit them the next day after work.

Kilang was still seething with irritation at the old man, but he decided that he would go because the little girl's case had to be sorted out with Aosenla. Though he was the sole authority in the Home, he had heard that some senior members of the staff were already asking questions about the status of the baby. When he arrived, he found Bendang and his wife in the drawing room along with their daughters watching television. It was their latest acquisition and the girls were enchanted with the gadget. They demurred when asked to leave the adults alone but Bendang was firm; either go out now or no television for two days. They were surprised at this sudden sternness but went out with long faces. Bendang immediately took over: he first told Kilang about the postponed trip and asked him to apologize to his friends. Secondly, he asked Aosenla to tell the doctor about his mother. Kilang was surprised at Bendang's behaviour, he was no longer the former patient, he was behaving as if he was conducting some Board Meeting. Oddly, this also reminded him of the old man at the last meeting when Bendang had cut such a sorry figure. But now, he seemed to have seized control as if stepping directly into his father's shoes.

Kilang was a person who seldom betrayed his emotions; so he told Bendang that though he was disappointed, he would inform his friends and wanted to add something else. But before he could elaborate, Bendang intervened and enquired if the physiotherapist in Jorhat could be requested to come for a month's stay to launch the programme, and at the same time teach his nurse the basic skills to carry on after he left. He added that he would be paid whatever he wanted. The doctor responded enthusiastically. He would go personally to fetch the man within the week. He also expressed his happiness at Bendang's positive response in the wake of the bereavement that the family had suffered so recently. Aosenla insisted that they all have tea together before they discussed the mother's case but Bendang wanted to be excused as he said he was feeling a bit tired and retired to his room.

This was the moment that Kilang had been praying for and as soon as he heard the door close on Bendang, he asked Aosenla what she was proposing to do about the baby. Calmly pouring a cup of tea for him, she replied, 'Doctor, let us not say anything now, but I promise I'll come tomorrow to your Home in the afternoon to fetch medicine for mother and then we will decide what is to be done about the baby. By the way, I hope she is all right?' At the mention of the baby, Kilang gave her a broad smile and said, 'Yes, she is fine and everybody loves her beautiful smile.' Aosenla understood how fond the good doctor had become of this waif. After he listened to Aosenla's account of the old woman's behaviour and other related physical symptoms, Kilang rose to go and said that he would wait for her in his office the next afternoon.

After the doctor left, Aosenla retired to her room, telling the maid not to let anyone in, not even her daughters. She needed time alone to think and plan for the child's future. The past few weeks had been hectic and extremely trying for all of them; first the preparations for the trip, then the sudden illness and death of her father-in-law, and now the care of the inconsolable mother-in-law. She had somehow managed to keep her composure and cope but all the while, a part of her mind was brooding over the fate of the child: what should she do? She suspected that if she confronted Bendang with the existence of his illegitimate granddaughter, he would surely deny everything and might even demand that Kilang turn her out of the Home. This would go contrary to her desire that the girl be kept in the Home not only for the excellent care she would receive there but also the more important reason that if she were there, it would allow Aosenla to monitor her progress.

Apart from these philanthropic and practical motives, another idea was taking shape in her mind regarding the child's future. For a very long time Aosenla did not want to articulate this idea which seemed so out of character for her. Inexplicably, she felt that it was now her duty to restore some measure of justice to the poor family. Increasingly her initial feelings of anger, resentment and outrage at being so cunningly manoeuvred into this marriage were now being tempered by thoughts of her own daughters' future. If she played the betrayed victim of the saga, where would it leave her daughters? How would they cope with the scandal and the heartbreak? Would seeking a personal vendetta against her husband be worth sacrificing their prospects in life? She wished she had someone to confide in and articulate her thoughts. The more she thought about it, the more convinced she became that it was she who would have to take the initiative. She did not realize it then, but the clarity of this conviction started a process which would eventually enable Aosenla to come into her own; Aosenla, the timid girl and submissive wife was gradually becoming Aosenla, the bold and decisive woman. It was as though she had been put through a trial by fire and emerged a wiser woman, who now saw her life in a more practical and objective way with all its varied twists and turns. For this woman from now on, nothing would be absolutely white or black.

The situation that presented itself was this: with the advent of this unwanted baby into the circle of her life, Aosenla's world became one that defied easy description. If her husband's accident caused them to live separately, though under the same roof, the new development further enlarged that separation and created a new twist as far as she was concerned. She felt as if she had been set adrift on a tiny canoe in a vast sea, as she desperately looked for light in the darkness. The burden of this knowledge now sat heavy in her heart. The fear that things could fall apart sobered Aosenla, and the intense soul-searching that went on in her mind convinced her that swallowing her pride was a indeed a very small price for preserving her marriage and safeguarding the future of her daughters.

Another thought briefly engaged her attention: the total irony of it all. The person who was responsible for creating this absurd situation was blithely unaware of the storm looming over his seemingly placid life. Aosenla, the victim of the initial cover-up, was now playing the role of an 'arranger', so that the past could be kept at bay. Meanwhile Bendang continued with the business of regaining control over his body so that he would not have to depend on anyone, least of all his wife. He had always striven to appear strong and manly before her and had decided that he should overcome any signs of weakness and be fit to play the role as head of the family. Little did he realize that such an image had long vanished from his wife's perception and she now viewed him totally differently. If he did not sense any obvious change in Aosenla's attitude towards him during their brief interactions, it was either due to the woman's extreme self-control or it could be that he was so obsessed with his total commitment to his own well-being that he failed to detect any telltale signs of change in anyone's behaviour or attitude. So the parallel existence of these two persons, brought together by fate and social manipulation continued. But the outward reality could not be more removed from the ever-widening inner estrangement felt mostly by Aosenla, though they remained tied in a seemingly ideal matrimony.

It was the force of this social bond that ultimately persuaded Aosenla to ignore the personal injustice done to her long ago. She knew that she was treading on very shaky ground as far as the baby's life was concerned; the need for utmost secrecy about her birth, and the search for plausible reasons for her eventual rehabilitation, all had to be executed with extreme care if the truth were to be kept hidden from everyone, including Bendang. First of all, the story about her coming to the Home should be believable; so the doctor would have to say that she was brought there because the mother was dead and the grandparents were too old to look after her. All true, but then what about the grandparents' identity? Aosenla planned on requesting the doctor to say that he was sworn not to reveal it because they wanted nothing to do with the child anymore. And thus the truth about her real parentage and the other related history, would be buried forever. It would also be made known that the grandfather who brought the child had given permission for adoption if the doctor could find loving parents. Aosenla was convinced that this background narrative would surely allay any misgiving about the baby's antecedents. Having chalked out this strategy, she went to bed with a lighter frame of mind and rested well.

The next day when Aosenla came to the Home, Kilang noticed that she looked cheerful; there were no visible signs of stress that he had seen on earlier occasions. After the mother-in-law's case was discussed and the medicines bought from the pharmacy, Kilang brought up the little girl's case. Aosenla listened to his concerns patiently and replied, 'Doctor, I want to proceed in a systematic manner and want to ask you a question. You keep on saying "baby" all the time, but what is her name? Didn't the grandfather give her a name?'

Kilang was taken aback; it was apparent that he had not thought of this at all. He looked at her blankly and remained silent. Aosenla apologized immediately, 'Please forgive me doctor, I asked because you met the old man and I thought that since names in our community are given to babies after five days of their births, I presumed that you were told of it. Now that we know that she does not have a proper name, can I suggest one?'

The doctor simply nodded and Aosenla continued, 'See, I have been thinking of just one name, what about calling her Tiajungla? It would be most appropriate because she is a child with a good fate. As you know, Tia in the Ao language means "fate" and "tajung" is the word for "good" from which the root word "jung" is taken and the female suffix "la" is added to create a complete name. And her short name can be Ajungla. How does that sound?'

Kilang thought for a while and said, 'It is a wonderful name and as you say, most appropriate for her. Tiajungla it is then and we'll call her Ajungla.'

The naming ceremony thus concluded in the baby's absence, Aosenla then briefed Kilang about what to say about her to his senior staff and record keeper. She also added that till such time as she saw fit, her name should not be linked to this case. She assured him that all the expenses for the child's upkeep would be paid by her and reiterated her earlier request about not saying anything to Bendang. As she was going out, almost as an afterthought, Aosenla stepped closer to Kilang and said a strange thing, 'Doctor, will you please hold back the permission for adoption from public knowledge just for a little while?' And without another word she walked out of his room. As she got into the car, the peon came running after her with her mother-in-law's medicines. She had forgotten to collect them from his table in her haste to depart.

After she went, Kilang sat in his office for a while trying to figure out this enigmatic woman. Today, as she was discussing the baby, he saw that she was calm, composed and exuded a confidence he had not seen in her so far. Gone was the timidity of earlier days; instead, she seemed to have become quite an assertive person. He thought to himself, 'I'll have to be careful with her, I should not allow her to affect me like this.' But he admitted to himself that she fascinated him as no other woman in his life had done thus far. He wondered at her total involvement with a baby that was the living testimony of her husband's perfidy; yet her main concern was for the child's welfare. And then he remembered the adoption question: why did she ask him to keep it a secret? Did she plan to adopt her into her family? Would it be the ultimate indictment of Bendang, even if he never learnt of the baby's real lineage? These baffling questions however only piqued his interest in this strange woman; but he also knew that he had to strictly go along with her plans in order to maintain his own neutrality in public and this irritated him. Why had he allowed himself to be manipulated by her? As he pondered over all that had happened after the baby's arrival, Kilang realized that there was a something that was drawing him more and more into the circle gradually created by Aosenla, and he was overcome by a sense of dread.

20

In sharp contrast to his interactions with Aosenla, Kilang's dealings with Bendang were practical and down-to-earth. The physiotherapist recommended by him was in fact an old friend whom Kilang had met while doing his post-graduate studies in Medicine in Dibrugarh Medical College. His name was Khagen Bora, a fellow PG student who had opted for physiotherapy. They got on very well together in the hostel and had kept in touch all these years. Khagen had set up his own clinic at Jorhat some five years ago and he seemed to be doing very well even though he had not yet been able to procure many modern gadgets as aids for his patients. But what he lacked in material aids, he supplemented with his skill in motivating his patients and helping them maintain their level of participation. Interestingly, he convinced them that pain was the first step to recovery and the acceptance and tolerance of pain was part of the process. Kilang had once stayed with him for a few days and what he saw amazed him. Unable to contain his curiosity, he asked Khagen where he learnt to do what he was doing because it appeared to him that his method combined psychology with physical exercises, topped off by salves and other medicines obtained from local herbs and roots. It was then that Khagen told him about his grandfather who had a reputation as a healer, though he never had any formal schooling and was only a simple farmer in the village.

He told Kilang that as a small boy, whenever they visited the village, he would watch people coming to the house with all sorts of ailments. Sometimes the old man would advise them to go to the government hospital in town, because he said he could not do anything for them with his simple methods. But the villagers would refuse to budge from the house until the old man at least touched the sick person or gave them some homemade ointment or medicine extracted from local plants and herbs. He would never take money from his patients, but as payment they would later bring vegetables, eggs, rice and on the rare occasion, a duck or a chicken. Khagen began to look forward to these annual visits to his grandfather's home and he told Kilang that it was during his high school years that he decided to study medicine and continue with his grandfather's noble profession.

One evening, as they sat in the verandah sipping tea, he turned to his visitor and said, 'You know, once I asked grandfather where he learnt to heal people. He smiled and said that it all started with a puppy.' 'A puppy?' Kilang asked. 'Yes, a puppy. Grandfather told us that one day as he was coming from the village pathsala, a puppy followed him and refused to leave the house, even though he was put out of the house many times. So he stayed and became grandfather's best friend, and followed him everywhere. Unfortunately one day, a bigger dog attacked him, and before grandfather could chase away the other dog, one of the puppy's legs got dislocated and there was a lot of blood. Grandfather came home with the injured puppy in his arms, crying as if his heart would break. When the father saw the little boy's face, he tried to soothe him and said that little animals always recovered from such accidents. But the boy was not to be comforted; he insisted his father take the puppy to a doctor and started to cry again. The father reluctantly took the boy with the injured puppy to the village healer. You know, when grandfather spoke of the moment when the old medicine-man put his hand on the puppy's injured leg and gave it a gentle twist, grandfather's eyes used to light up as if it was his own moment of healing! Then he would smile and tell me how that little whimpering bundle bounced out of his arms and began to trot around in the room. He told me that it was almost like magic. That is why, he said, from that day on, he came to the medicine-man's house every day to learn from him this 'magic'. And I, Khagen Bora, learnt to love this magic from my grandfather and that is why I became a doctor. I am sure that grandfather would have been very proud of me if he were alive today. Once, during my student days in the medical college, I asked him how he managed to heal so many people without any formal knowledge of medical science. He smiled at me and said, "Dear grandson, I'll tell you a secret. If you want to heal a body, heal the mind first." It struck me as the most important lesson of my life and I have tried to do that with every patient.' It was an extraordinary story, and Kilang looked at his friend with renewed respect and pride.

When Dr Khagen Bora was brought to Bendang's house, everyone took to him immediately because of his amiable nature. He wasted no time and set up the equipment in a spare room, telling Bendang that they were going to start the exercises the very next day. There was an aura of confidence and firmness about him, which became apparent to Bendang, and he accepted the unspoken challenge offered to him. At first, the pain was excruciating when the almost unused muscles were massaged and mauled by firm hands. Though the broken bones in the leg were almost healed, a sort of stiffness had set in because he'd been confined to the wheelchair and the bed. Taking the first tentative step, holding on to a rail, created so much pain that Bendang doubled over, howling that his back was broken. Dr Bora ignored the protest and calmly said, 'one more step'. The first day Bendang managed only four steps and refused to try any more. The doctor did not insist and only said, 'Massage time 5 o' clock'. The only relief for Bendang was that he was alone with the doctor and the nurse; Aosenla did not see him in these humiliating circumstances. The doctor would not entertain any of Bendang's many excuses to either postpone or give up the gruelling routine, and his days alternated between the pain of the exercises and the intervals of much needed lie-downs in between. But amazingly, his body began to respond well to the therapy and he was beginning to believe that he would soon recover complete control of his limbs. If he had to bear these bouts of pain for that, he said to himself, so be it. Of one thing he was very sure, he would no longer give in to the pain but would overcome his disability one step at a time.

Aosenla was happy to see the determination in his eyes, and his optimism seemed to have roused the family from their stupor as well. There was a new sense of hope, and even the girls sometimes wanted to join the father in his exercise room; but there were strict rules regarding that room. No one, not even his wife, could enter it when the sessions were on. So the girls skipped and ran about in the compound while the more serious push-ups and runs on the walker were being executed amidst groans and curses inside closed doors.

For Aosenla however, these were only momentary diversions from other important commitments; she now saw herself as leading a double life: the public life of a dutiful wife, mother and daughter-in-law, and the other life of a woman trying to create a balance between a public truth and a more sinister private truth about her family. The individuality that Aosenla had so zealously tried to guard all her adult life, was now somewhat fragmented by the different roles that she had to play in public. In trying to juggle the different priorities she had often to resort to subterfuge in order to keep her two lives apart, lest an unguarded remark or a careless slip unmask her and destroy the façade of normalcy that she had so assiduously constructed. It was no wonder then that she was at times assailed by doubts about the rightness or wrongness of her methods of dealing with her predicament. But she could not yet fully articulate, or would not acknowledge that these were the inevitable compromises that one had to make in order to live in a society that put so much emphasis on normalcy and propriety.

Meanwhile, in the physiotherapy room, Khagen was engaged in a process of gentle probing. Between sessions, he would initiate conversations with Bendang in order to draw him out. And, in the most seemingly innocuous moments, he would slip in comments in order to make the patient introspect. For example, one day while talking about the accident, he casually asked Bendang why it had occurred: who was driving and was there a mechanical failure? Or was he under the influence of alcohol? The first two questions were easy for Bendang. He said he was driving and there was no mechanical failure. He emphasized that he was a good driver and he took personal care of the car. But when it came to the second question, Bendang began to give excuses: no, he was not drunk, he had only been drinking beer with friends; what he omitted to add was that they had drunk beer when the whiskey ran out and he, as an experienced drinker, knew how destructive that cocktail could be. Bora kept quiet for a while. Bendang sensed his disbelief in the silence, and burst out, 'Ok, so what if we had drunk a little whiskey earlier?' Bora simply smiled and said, 'Now you know what happens when you do that.' They never spoke of the accident again, but the doctor kept communication with his patient at a very friendly level and eventually they started to talk about cars, and Bendang blurted out that what hurt him most was the fact that he was afraid that he would never be able to drive again. Bora saw how anguished Bendang looked when he said that but instead of offering words of assurance, he began to talk about new cars coming to the market and how beautiful the new models were. He added that the day of the jeep was over; it was now the small cars that ruled the streets everywhere.

What he was doing was to remind Bendang of his love of cars, and by talking about the new entrants to the market, he was stoking his will to become fully fit so that he could drive again. Bendang asked his news vendor to get magazines on cars and began to read up on the new models. He pored over the details as if there was some remedy for him in the pictures and texts. And then one fine morning, when they were about to start their session, he told the doctor that he wanted to buy a new car and asked Bora to contact the dealer in Jorhat. But Bora looked at him skeptically and said, 'Not yet, you need to gain more control over your muscles and the mind-body co-ordination is yet to be perfected.' Bendang's mood changed, but the therapist was adamant; he pushed him hard to achieve the level of rehabilitation that he thought adequate for re-entry into his old way of life. The exercises continued for another two weeks.

Aosenla did not seem to have any say in what went on in the exercise room, but for her too, this period turned out to be one in which her attitude towards her mother-in-law changed. It also marked an important stage in the restoration of a sort of balance. The events of the past year had altered the prism through which she viewed life; she decided that there were no clear boundaries between the colours, only varying shades in the truths, half-truths and lies. Imperceptively but inevitably, she was growing into the matriarch of the family, and everyone, the servants, Bendang and Kilang, looked to her when it came to important decisions. For example, when Bendang wanted to purchase another car, he consulted her about what colour she wanted. She, in turn, asked her daughters. Both of them shouted at once: 'red' and so it was; after a fortnight a brand new Maruti 800 was driven into the compound by the driver who had to fetch it all the way from the dealers in Jorhat.

She often thought of her mother-in-law who had lived in the shadow of a strong man. She began to wonder if the old woman knew anything about her son's past and whether her husband had taken her into confidence about the cover-up and the obvious payoff to the pregnant girl's father. She concluded that he had not, it was just not in his character. Aosenla found that the woman, who seemed to be her antagonist from the day she stepped into the family, had now become an object of her pity. The old woman was beginning to confide in her more; she told Aosenla how she had saved a lot of money from housekeeping and from the money the children gifted her when they visited. She insisted on showing her the secret places where she had stashed away her treasure; they were not very secret though unless one considered bottoms of drawers and shoe-boxes to be secret places. Once in a while, she would take a few bundles and offer them to Aosenla, who politely persuaded her to keep them where they were, promising to ask her if she needed money. Once, she was almost tempted to accept a bundle when she realized that she had to send some amount to Kilang urgently for Ajungla's upkeep. But she resisted the urge and helped the old woman to stash it away along with the other bundles. She had to deal with her mother-in-law as though she was a child, and it amazed Aosenla how quickly their roles had been reversed. She thought she needed more time to really understand her mother-in-law's earlier actions as the matriarch of a powerful family who had seemed so arrogant and self-possessed only a year ago.

With Kilang however, it was different. After all, he did not have the opportunity, or the familiarity to share his private thoughts with her. During the frequent meetings with him on account of her mother-in-law's condition, Aosenla began to notice that he often looked distracted, as if he was worried about something. She told herself it was probably to do with the recent illness from which he was recovering. Then other matters claimed her attention and she forgot about him and did not bother to call him for about a week. But at the back of her mind she was acutely aware that sooner, rather than later, she had to find a permanent solution for Ajungla's future, and this could be done only in consultations with Kilang.

In the meantime, Bendang's physiotherapy sessions were going well: he could now walk slowly with the help of a walking stick and so the hated waste-deposit trays were banished from his room. He was eating better and some colour had returned to his face. But it was apparent that the faint traces of lacerations on his face would never disappear. Dr Bora had by now become a trusted friend and they were on first name terms. The new car turned out to be the perfect stimulus for accelerating the healing process because the doctor understood how much of an outdoor person his patient was, and the prospect of driving the symbol of mobility and freedom reposing in his garage would keep up his spirits. He was not exactly a trained psychologist but by studying human infirmities and facilitating not only physical rehabilitation but also some amount of mental well-being, he had learnt the importance of motivation in achieving the desired goal. It needed no theories; only genuine sympathy and understanding of the victims of trauma.

The doctor's tenure was soon over and he made preparations for going back to his own work. He had been happy in this household, and he was returning hugely satisfied with the results of his efforts. The pay he received was also handsome and there was an added bonus too. Bendang was sad to see him go but he was confident that he could now manage on his own. Besides, Hariba would carry on with the new techniques that he had learnt from Dr Bora. When the time came, a plain handshake marked the moment of farewell and as he climbed onto the jeep, the doctor turned to his patient and shouted, 'Hey, Bendang, bring your family in that red toy of yours to my house during the Pujas; I would like to try it out myself,' and giving him a mock salute, disappeared through the gate. The holidays he mentioned were just two months away; Bendang understood that the doctor was giving him a deadline.

21

The departure of Dr Bora from the household meant that a major relocation was inevitable: the most important question was whether Bendang would opt to return to the old bedroom to share it with his wife. Or, Aosenla wondered, would he prefer the relative freedom of his rehabilitation room? And of course she had to ask herself too: would she welcome him back to the room that had now become her sanctuary? And more importantly, could she openly oppose any move on his part to return and declare that she preferred the present arrangement? This uncertainty about their attitude to each other became a crisis of another kind for Aosenla. If, she ruefully thought, the baby had not intruded into their lives, she was sure that she would have coped with whatever decision Bendang took about moving or not moving back. The existence of the child, and Aosenla's own complicity in sheltering her in the Home, made it much harder for her to ease back into their earlier relationship. And she was no longer sure she would be able to remain in control if they were to go back to their old life.

The more she pondered over this dilemma, the more afraid she became. True, the traumatic experience of losing her child had been a setback but it was a personal one, and one she had somehow overcome. But this time round, she was not sure how she would cope. Though many people were involved in this story and were responsible for the developments, they were ironically blissfully unaware of what had happened or what was likely to happen to the lot of them. Some, like Bendang's father and the little girl's mother, were no longer there; but Bendang was alive and most likely living with a false sense of comfort that things were all right. And now that he was fully recovered, he might come back to their room to resume his rightful place as master of the house and expect to be reinstated as her husband in every sense of the word.

As if he sensed some reluctance in his wife about his return to the master bedroom, Bendang continued with his exercises and never once mentioned the subject. In the meantime, Aosenla, in order perhaps to avoid facing the real problem, initiated a massive renovation plan for both the houses, beginning with theirs first. One evening, she called for a family meeting and everyone assembled in the drawing room. After a while, her mother-in-law was escorted into the room. Then Aosenla triumphantly produced a trader's colour sheet and began to talk about how the houses had not been painted in years and how certain rooms badly needed refurbishing and so on. To the others' great surprise, the old woman vociferously supported her daughter-in-law's proposal. Without further prompting, the two girls immediately began to argue about the colour schemes for their rooms, leaving Bendang absolutely outnumbered and voiceless. It was however a pleasant gathering, and after consuming a lot of cakes and biscuits they dispersed. For the first time in a long while, his mother turned to Bendang and spoke to him, asking him to escort her to her room in the big house. He stayed with her for quite a while. When he came back, he went straight to their old room where Aosenla was sorting out some clothes, and taking hold of her hands he said, 'I will arrange for everything you need for the project, but on one condition; you do our room first so that I can move back as soon as it's done.' Aosenla had not anticipated this and she was a bit annoyed, but she managed to smile at him and murmured, 'I was wondering when you would say this.'

After his departure, she was overcome by a sense of temporary relief as well as dread. The job would take at least two weeks, but afterwards, they would have to be in the same room. The thing that worried her was that this man, her husband, was not the same man she had known him to be. His image was tarnished beyond redemption in her eyes and her constant torment would be to pretend that all was well between them. This thought made Aosenla sick to her stomach and she had to sit down on the bed to gather her wits. She spent an extremely agitated evening and refused to have any dinner, saying that she had a terrible headache.

The renovation work began in right earnest; many labourers were engaged and the compound was soon strewn with step-ladders, paint brushes, tins of paint. Sometimes the whole scenario looked like a holi party gone wrong. But gradually the work was completed in the smaller house and the workers moved to the big house. It was here that the trouble started. The old mother-in-law refused to allow them to enter saying that there were many valuable things that might get lost. No amount of reasoning would allay her fears; she bolted the main doors and shouted at the workers to go away. In desperation, Aosenla asked the workers to paint at least the exterior of the house. At first they refused to touch the big house but she persuaded them, and grudgingly and with in ill-disguised antagonism towards the old woman (they called her 'witch') they somehow managed to give the older house a fresh look.

With the completion of this project, the dreaded moment was upon Aosenla. But when she had thought of

Bendang's return to their room, she had resolved that the first step would have to come from him. So she went about her household chores as before, personally supervising her mother-in-law's bath times, changing the bed linen and making sure that she ate her meals properly. Outwardly, she was the picture of a devoted mother, wife and daughter-in-law. It was only when the day's duties were done, that the inner turmoil would take hold of her and she would toss and turn on the huge bed, grateful that she was still by herself. Her rational self told her that she needed to swallow her pride, suppress her ego and move forward for the sake of her daughters. She resisted this course of action but one night she suddenly realized that in all the happenings of the last month or so, an important factor had escaped her attention.

In less than a year's time, her elder daughter Chubala would be leaving home to begin her college life. She would have to move into a hostel. Her second daughter Narola too would be completing her tenth grade and this feisty girl was already hinting that unlike her sister, she would like to go out for her eleventh and twelfth grades. Somehow the prospect of having both the daughters out of the house at more or less the same time brought a chill to Aosenla's heart. Just the two of them, she and her husband, would be left in the sprawling house. For the first time in her married life she was truly afraid, but of what or whom she did not quite know. The only consolation was that there were several months before this actually happened and so she began to plan for that eventuality.

If Aosenla had anticipated any dramatics in her husband's eventual return to their old bedroom, she was disappointed. In fact, when it happened, it was something of an anti-climax. It was on an evening when she was least expecting it. After dinner, her daughters spent some time with her watching something on television, and then, having said goodnight, they noisily trooped back to their own rooms. Aosenla dawdled over her evening rituals, telling herself how peaceful it was to have so much calm and privacy. But after only a few moments when she heard a timid knock on her door, she stiffened, wishing it to be someone else and not her husband. Before she could respond, the door was pushed open and Bendang entered, in his nightshirt and pyjamas. She was at a complete loss about what to say; she simply gazed at him as though from a great distance. She'd had no time to prepare and she stood there with dismay writ large on her face. What she saw in the man standing on the threshold was a man who had paled because of his long confinement indoors; the old robust look had not yet returned though she could see that he would soon display that shade. The man standing upright, without the benefit of the familiar walking stick was another image that contrasted with her idea of her invalid husband. But of one thing she became immediately aware; it was the old Bendang who was not fazed by her unwelcome silence. His demeanour did not change; he simply nodded and went to his accustomed side of the bed and slipped under the covers. Looking at her intently for some time, he simply said goodnight and turned his face away. Aosenla understood that he wanted to demonstrate to her that the decision to come back was entirely his prerogative whether she welcomed it or not. For her it was like reliving an altered version of their first night; this time round the event was stripped of any excitement or romantic expectations from either player. With a resigned sigh, she too finished her night-time rituals and curled up in her corner of the big bed to mull over the future with this man who now seemed to have become a total stranger. Lying awake for a long time after he started snoring, she contemplated how she would behave with in the future with him now that she had become privy to the dark secret of his past.

In the rest of the household however, Bendang's return to his old room was viewed differently; it meant that sahib was now fully recovered and they could forget about the terrible accident. Everything was back to normal and they were happy. In no time, all of Bendang's wardrobe came back to the original cupboards and drawers in the big room, and very soon it felt like he had never been away from it at all. Even for the girls, their father shifting back to the big bedroom seemed so normal that they did not comment on it except for Narola saying, 'Good, now we can talk to you both at the same time.' If the new arrangement created any uncertainty for anyone, it was for Hariba, the male nurse who instinctively knew that his employment was at an end in this household. And sure enough, at the end of the month he was sent off with a handsome bonus. There was however an important addition to Bendang's wardrobe: three walking sticks that he had procured during his convalescence. He wanted them propped up by his bedside table at all times though he had no use for them now. Once, when Aosenla suggested that they should be stored either inside or atop the big wardrobe, he almost shouted at her not to do so. They remained where he wanted them to be and even the servants were warned not to touch or dislodge them from the space by his side of the bed. By and by Bendang had a beautiful glass showcase made of teakwood and his precious walking sticks were securely locked inside and pushed against a section of the wall which was in his direct line of vision from his side of the bed.

Bendang's move back to his old bedroom however, seemed to have generated a new energy in him and created a kind of dynamic in their relationship that Aosenla had not felt before. She was right in thinking of him as a 'total stranger' but not in the way she had seen him when he made his first appearance in their bedroom. It was as if his recovery had given the entire household a new lease of life; the servants were chirpier and exuded a greater willingness to perform their duties without sour faces and mumbled complaints. In the old house, even her mother-in-law seemed to have woken from slumber and become more active in the house. She began to take more interest in her surroundings. But one thing remained constant: her cantankerousness. She scolded the gardener for not pulling out the weeds on time and turning up the soil around the roots of the plum saplings. She complained to Aosenla that the maid did not scour the pots and pans properly and wanted her to inspect them. She claimed that her bedclothes had not been aired for months and that she was sleeping on sheets several weeks dirty. Aosenla was amazed at this turn of events, especially the new interest and energy in the old woman. She also knew that what she said about her bedclothes was not true because she herself saw to it that they were aired every weekend, and the sheets were changed every two days. For a change, she was not irritated with her mother-in-law for the exaggeration, but intrigued by her renewed energy and concluded that it was Bendang's recovery that was responsible for this.

Her daughters reacted a bit differently. While Narola was happy that both parents could be spoken to at the same time, Chubala simply smiled and hugged her mother and went about her way. While Aosenla was still trying to absorb the changes she decided, one afternoon, to sort out her clothes, something she had been meaning to do for a while. As she was engaged in the task, Chubala tiptoed into the room and sat down on the bed. After the usual enquiries about her day at school, Aosenla returned to her task. But after a while, she became aware that her daughter was unusually quiet and felt that she was struggling with something she wanted to say. Aosenla pushed the heap of clothes aside and turned to Chubala. When the daughter remained quiet with her head bowed down, she moved closer to her and took both her hands in hers and asked, 'What is it, darling, did you want to say something to me?' Chubala was silent. Aosenla waited patiently because she knew that it had taken a lot of courage for her introvert daughter to come this far. The mother stroked her daughter's face gently, at which Chubala broke into sobs.

Aosenla was concerned: what could have caused this calm person to sob like this? She persisted, 'Tell me Chuba, what is worrying you, have you done something wrong or is it something someone said that has upset you so much?' Chubala's sobs slowly subsided and composing herself, she started to talk, 'You see mummy, I have been observing you and daddy these past months since he moved out of the big bedroom and I can see that you were not as before, both of you. Even after he recovered, he continued to stay away and I feared that you two were going to get divorced.'

Aosenla was stunned: divorce! Even with the dark knowledge that had been thrust on her, she had not considered that option even for a moment and here was her young daughter being burdened by the threat of a divorce because of her apparent apathy towards her husband, which must have become obvious in spite of her efforts to hide it. Gently, she put her arms around her daughter and told her in an emotionally charged voice, 'Never, my darling, we will never do that to you and your sister.' Chubala took her mother's face in her hands and said, 'I know now because you are together again and I had actually come to tell you how happy we both are because of it.' She got up abruptly and said with an effort at normalcy, 'Ok then, I'll also see which dresses I want to get rid of so that all the clothes can be given to some needy people. But I can assure you mummy, Narola will hang on to everything she has; you know how she is!' With that flippant remark about her sister, Chubala gave her mother a hug and went out of the room.

After she had gone, Aosenla sat on the floor and thought about what had just happened; she was flabbergasted. Were her feelings towards her husband so transparent so that her sensitive daughter had clearly recognized the alienation and was worried they may divorce? If the young girl could sense the growing emotional distance she felt towards her husband, what about the man himself? She could no longer concentrate on what she was doing and, shoving everything inside a big laundry bag, she deposited it inside the storage space for odds and ends and walked out to the garden to compose herself. Once there, she thought she may as well look into her mother-in-law's complaints about the state of the garden. To her surprise, she saw that everything was in order, the plants properly trimmed, the weeds cleaned out, so she returned to the bedroom to think about what Chubala had just said. She had to admit that her daughter was no longer an innocent girl, she had now come of age emotionally. She'd seen and understood what was happening between her parents.

Aosenla now asked herself if she could live up to the assurance she had so spontaneously given her daughter. Could she restore some kind of balance in her relationship with her husband? All along, she had sensed that her life and desires were not entirely her own; that she did not actually own herself. She was merely a part of a whole, the preservation of which required her to subsume herself. It was a big challenge and she had to summon all her strength to be equal to it. Another thought struck her; had there been any visible reaction when she regained her health after the ordeal of the third pregnancy? She could not remember whether anyone in the house had shown any signs of relief. Was it, she wondered, because she was only the wife and not the man of the house? But she told herself that perhaps it was because her husband's plight was more serious and posed a greater threat to the entire family. It would be unfair to compare the two incidents, so she gave up that course of thinking. But there remained a niggling doubt in her mind about this.

22

After Bendang's almost full recovery, Dr Kilang came to visit him one evening and in the course of the conversation, he casually remarked that some people were trying to create problems for him in the running of the Home. Bendang was surprised and asked, 'Why, is it about money? Are the workers unhappy over their wages? Actually, I've always wanted to ask you how you manage to run it with only your own resources; and now that prices are escalating and it must be really hard for you. Tell me, how can I be of help?'

Kilang was at first stunned by the directness in Bendang's queries. He had known him to be a reticent person, always measuring his words when in company, but today he sounded like a new person -- more forthright and assertive. He wondered if he could confide in him and, knowing that he could not turn to any other person for help, he reluctantly began to reveal his worries to Bendang.

As he began his story, Kilang tried to be as casual as possible, but it became increasingly clear that the good doctor was far more troubled than he cared to admit. There was a slight tremor in his voice when he started to talk and he held back after the first few words. But Bendang persisted with his probing and urged that he tell him what had caused this great worry. At this encouragement, Kilang began to speak in a calmer voice and there was no stopping him once he started his story.

'You see the Home is built on land given to me by my father. You may remember that he was a minor functionary of the government and when he retired, his Department Head presented him with this bit of land in recognition of his long and commendable service. It was not a big piece of land; it also had a sloping boundary, which further diminished its value. After I decided to start the Home, I was looking for a piece of land to build it and it was then that my father gifted it to me.

'When I started this project, I had a bit saved from my salary as a government doctor and I invested all of it in the building. But the overhead costs of staff salaries and medicine alone far exceed whatever returns there are from patients and inmates. Can you imagine, some people want to pay me in paddy or livestock! Which medical supplier will accept a pig or two as payment? And even the staff expects hard cash at the end of each month. Of course there are a few workers who have agreed to wait for their salaries for a few months, but I cannot make them suffer on account of my own difficulties. So you see, the only solution that I can see is to sell the entire establishment to anyone willing to pay me the right price so that I can clear all my debts to the staff as well as the medicine and equipment suppliers.'

Heaving a long sigh, Kilang stretched out on the deep sofa he was sitting on and covered his face with his hands as if he was ashamed of what he had just revealed. Bendang looked at the doctor for a long time; he had known this man for nearly twenty years now, though he could not say that he really 'knew' him as a close friend. But deep in his mind, he had always held a grudging respect towards this unassuming person for his dedicated service to the poor and destitute of the town. He had initially frowned on Aosenla's interest in the doctor's good work; why it was so he could not explain even to himself. Was he jealous of his wife's admiration for the doctor? Did he feel that Kilang's altruism shamed his own pursuit of wealth? But as their association developed through the years, he began to recognize his quiet strength and his commitment. And now he could see what a struggle it had been for the mild-mannered doctor to hold on to his dream.

Bendang suddenly felt humbled in the presence of such a determined and selfless man and wanted to reach out and be of some help. He got up and began to speak, 'Hey, hey, Kilang, look, why are you so dejected? Surely, nothing is lost yet and the Home is doing all right. Do not think that you are alone in this, after all the Home belongs to the entire community and I for one, will do anything to keep it going, and with you at the helm. Give me a few days and I will think of a way to lighten your burden; and I thank you for being so honest about your circumstances. Come; let us go out for some fresh air.' So saying, he guided the doctor out to the lawn where they sipped tea and talked about other things. Kilang felt increasingly uncomfortable and did not finish the tea in his cup. After a few desultory exchanges, Kilang excused himself and left. Though Bendang vaguely noticed the change in Kilang, his concern was more with the financial difficulties of the doctor and he briefly pondered over his own spontaneous response to what Kilang had said. After a while, he decided that he would make some enquiries first before he broached the subject with his wife.

Kilang went home in a very confused state of mind: most of all he was angry with himself for baring his soul, of all persons to Bendang, a man towards whom he had always entertained a certain distance. He was not sure why he felt this way. After all, Bendang had been his patient for a considerable length of time and usually the doctor-patient relationship often matures into one of mutual trust. But in their case, though the initial stiffness and formality had somehow eased, there still remained a strong tentativeness in their attitude to each other. It is also true that in such situations, the doctor usually had the upper hand over the patient. But here too, Kilang was aware that he could never feel that way with this patient because he was outside the elite circle where Bendang belonged. And now he felt that by his ill-advised revelation about his financial problems, he had further denigrated himself in Bendang's esteem.

When he thought about it, he became truly mortified. 'What possessed me to do it and what good will it do?' he asked himself. All this whining and complaining about his affairs to a man, who had, he remembered now, listened to him more and more with an academic interest rather than any genuine human feeling. He recalled that in the beginning Bendang did say that he would do all in his power to save the Home as it was meant for the community etc., but as the conversation turned to details of the land and its size, Bendang did not once ask what would happen to the inmates of the Home should the ownership pass on to another; his queries about the Home site from then onwards seemed to be focused entirely on its viability as a piece of real estate. The doctor was now convinced that he had done more harm than good to himself and his beloved mission by sharing his worries with such a man.

When he reached his office he looked at the piles of paper on his table and, as though to undo what he had done a while ago, he began to attack the paper mess and started stacking them on a shelf, which was already cluttered with old invoices and receipts. In the middle of this haphazard attempt at a semblance of tidiness, the doctor was suddenly seized by a new thought; it was so abrupt and absurd that he nearly threw the bundle of papers that he was holding through the open window. He stopped in mid-throw and dumped the bundle on the floor and sat down to compose his thoughts. At first, the idea seemed so bizarre and ludicrous that he burst into a dry cackle.

'The irony of it all,' he kept repeating, 'the irony of it all! Imagine, here is a man with a dark past which has come home to roost in the person of this waif now sleeping peacefully in this Home, and the Home is tottering on the brink of collapse! And I've gone and blabbed to this very person who, but for the intervention of his distraught wife and my own complicity in the cover-up, would have been by now exposed for the kind of man he is. I have acted like a colossal fool; first by being an accomplice to the cover-up and now revealing to Bendang how close I am to being bankrupt. O wretched me,' he cried and dashed out of the room only to dash back to put off the lights and lock the doors and windows.

After a restless and troubled night, the doctor woke with a somewhat lighter heart. 'Amazing,' he thought, 'how God's own daylight can make even the worst crisis of one's life seem more bearable.' This fleeting sense of relief however, did not last long because he now realized that so far, his concern had centred mainly upon the new equation between himself and Bendang. Aosenla's name came to mind only when he thought of their 'conspiracy' but afterwards it simply vanished, it was as if she did not exist at all. And this thought jolted him out of his complacency. He asked himself if he had, in some way, betrayed her by making Bendang privy to his problems. But he had always had a somewhat ambivalent attitude towards her, one that was somehow tinged with a bit of dread. As soon as he articulaed the word 'dread' he recalled that incident in his office when he had, on an impulse, gone and sat close to her. He still recalled the look in Aosenla's eyes, which did not reveal anything – the eyes looked dead. He had been haunted by that look for a long time and constantly berated himself for his unseemly behaviour. He also cautioned himself to be more careful in his dealings with this enigmatic woman. Even now, as the question of betrayal came into his mind, he realized that in spite of his best efforts, his feelings for her had not changed. Maybe because of this he had decided that he would try to find a solution to his problems without Aosenla's involvement if necessary, because he believed that only then would his survival and that of his family be assured. He was surprised at his lack of concern for Aosenla's feelings, though she was so totally and irrevocably entangled in the inner mess of his Home. Yet during the most desperate moments in the night, he had completely blanked her out of his mind because she had to be kept outside the circle of his intimate personal environment. He could not afford even the slightest deviation from social correctness if he were to survive. 'So this is what the struggle for survival means,' he said to himself, as he continued to think of ways to overcome his enormous burden.

Aosenla's worries were of a different nature; she had discovered her husband in the drawing room long after the doctor had gone and, sensing his mood, she asked him if he was all right. 'Yes,' Bendang replied curtly, but immediately softened his tone and said, 'See, I want to sort out some ideas by myself. You go on with whatever you're doing, I'll join you later. But don't wait up for dinner.' She looked at him for a while without saying anything and then went out. She was suddenly alarmed; had Kilang said something to Bendang to send him into such a mood? Had he somehow found out about the orphan's presence in the Home? What would she say if he confronted her with the demand to know the truth? Could she lie to her husband? And what if the doctor had already told him the truth about the baby, where would that leave her? These two actors were tied together by the secret they shared and now Bendang too had been drawn into it though his involvement was of a very different nature. It had nothing to with his intimate self or his tenuous relationship with either Kilang or Aosenla; for him it was not the harrowing burden it was for the other two. For him, it was purely a financial matter, the hard question being whether he ought to invest in Kilang's floundering Home or leave him to his fate. Bendang knew that without a substantial rescue offer from someone, Kilang would surely have to give up his precious Home; but strangely, that prospect did not seem to disturb him at all. For him, the Home and its finances had simply become a puzzling piece of pure mathematics, and if the calculations indicated a plus, he would surely take the plunge. Having made this cold decision, he went into the bedroom where he found that his wife had taken her usual position on her side of the bed facing the wall. He knew the signs so he quietly went to bed without bothering about dinner.

The next morning, Aosenla woke up with a headache and refused to budge even when the girls came in to say bye before going to school. Chubala thought that her mother was acting up because she was to leave home soon to start her college life. So she tiptoed to her and whispered: 'Remember you promised to take me to your tailor today for my clothes for college, so be ready when I come home. And oh, I will come home early today because the farewell party will take only an hour or so.' This reminder jolted Aosenla out of her lethargy and she tried to remain calm, and began to gather all the materials that she had bought for her daughters. She then called up her tailor to request him to keep some free time for them. The prospect of this excursion somehow lightened Aosenla's mind but she decided that at the very first opportunity she would ask Kilang about his meeting with her husband the previous night.

While Aosenla tried to ignore her worries by spending more time than necessary at the tailor's, Bendang set his plan in motion. First, he called a good friend of his who worked in the only bank in town, and where he knew Kilang also banked, and asked him to enquire discreetly about the doctor's financial status. When the figures were presented to him in the evening, he discovered that the doctor had been honest to the last paisa. The next move was to obtain an appraisal of the land and built-in property that housed the Home. He learnt that when the Home was first built, it was considered to be outside the main plan of the town. But after these many years, it was fast becoming a central location as the town had expanded considerably in all directions and was heading towards becoming a municipality. So Kilang's Home was now on prime land with enough vacant space for future expansion. Bendang was overjoyed; he thought that he should offer the doctor a reasonable amount and relieve him of his worries. This put him in a very good mood and he decided that he should approach Kilang without delay.

23

In the meantime, unknown to any of the three players, there was a newcomer in town who had come expressly to verify the reputation of the Home, which had spread beyond the small town. He was a man of the church, whose headquarters were located in Calcutta, and his name was Reverend David Ponraj. He was escorted by a former inmate of the Home who had gone on to study in the seminary at Serampore, and was now working as an evangelist and school teacher in a remote village church in the 24 Parganas district of West Bengal. On his way home for a short vacation, he had met the Reverend at a student gathering in Calcutta where the evangelist named Sunup Jamir was speaking about his life in Dr Kilang's Home, and testifying how this gentle doctor was not only saving orphans and abandoned children but also helping promising students by finding sponsors for further education. He declared, 'I am not the only one who has been helped by this servant of God; there are two more of my classmates who are studying medicine and will soon join Dr Kilang in his Home. Let us all pray for him and his Home because I've lately heard rumours that he is facing some financial problems. When I meet him, I shall tell him of your support.' The Reverend was intrigued by this bit of information and after the service was over, he sought out Sunup and wanted to know more about the Home. Seeing his keen interest, Sunup blurted out, 'Reverend, why don't you come with me and see for yourself what this wonderful man is doing?' The Reverend was taken aback; the directness of the invitation was almost like a challenge and he did not know how to react. He had never been to this part of the country and what little he knew about it was not very flattering.

But he was a seasoned man of the church and a firm believer in the mysterious ways in which God dealt with human affairs. He recalled that only a month ago, a friend of his had told him that he wanted to donate part of his inheritance to a worthy humanitarian cause and had requested the Reverend to help him in this search. But his friend was from Tamil Nadu and the Reverend had told him that there were enough 'good causes' in his own state and he could donate to any one of his own choice. Now, if he were to suggest that his friend help Kilang out of his present crisis, would he agree to send his money to this small town in Nagaland, a town he may not even have heard of? This new idea now suddenly became a real challenge for the Reverend and he thought that the only way to learn about this doctor's mission, and if need be, convince his friend to donate his money to this unheard-of Home, would be to go and see for himself. Having made this decision, the Reverend turned to Sunup and said, 'I am coming with you to meet your Dr Kilang,' and that is how he landed in the town after four harrowing days of travel by train and bus. If he was exhausted physically, he was also drained out mentally: it was as if he'd landed on another planet. The vast differences between his own environment and the strange one to which he had so impulsively come seemed overwhelming at first; the people, the language, the food, the topography and the ease with which men and women interacted both at home and outside, were all alien. He needed a day or two to take in the strangeness of it all. But once he met Kilang and listened to his account of how he started the humble Home with nothing but a vision, the Reverend understood that he was meeting a man who truly personified selfless service to humanity and deserved to be called a 'true servant of God'. He thought, 'We, who go to seminaries and master doctrines and only preach, need to learn humility and sacrifice from such a person like Dr Kilang.' It was clear in his mind that he would tell his friend back in Tamil Nadu about the wonderful work of this humble doctor and suggest that he give his donation to the Home. Throughout their meeting, Kilang did not display any worry or anxiety and the Reverend also did not say anything about his real reason for visiting this remote area of the country in mid-summer. But as he thought about his encounter with this unassuming doctor on his journey back home, he was convinced that God had brought him to this strange place for a purpose and that he was going to fulfil that purpose with his friend's help.

Though Kilang enjoyed the Reverend's visit, he did not attach any special significance to it because there were always plenty of visitors who came and some also left small donations and gifts for the children. For him it was just one such visit, pleasant while it lasted, but now he was back to his old routine of tending to patients and racking his brains about the bills once more piling up on his table. It had been two weeks since his confession to Bendang about his financial problems and he was still castigating himself for what he saw as his weakness. There had been no communication from that house so far. In the meantime, a small insurance policy had matured and he was able to clear the most urgent bills for medicine. But much more was needed and he had to find a saviour very soon, he thought cynically. He also remembered Bendang saying, 'Give me a few days and I will think of a way to lighten your burden.' The 'few days' had now stretched to almost a month and though he was sorely tempted, Kilang resolved that he would not be the one to remind Bendang. 'Let him come with an offer if he's interested,' he told himself. 'I'll not go to him; I'll not behave like a beggar. I am sure that God will show me a way this time too, as He has always done.'

Though the prospects of the home site were positive, something held Bendang back from making a definitive move towards acquiring the property. That is why he did not mention anything about his conversation with Kilang to his wife. Aosenla, however, was totally preoccupied with the imminent departure of her elder daughter. While the preparations were going on, Narola was sulking on the sidelines because all the attention was now on Chubala. A typical domestic scene, Aosenla mused. But she did, from time to time, wonder what had transpired between her husband and Kilang and why the two men were behaving as if she did not exist at all. It really bothered her that all the details of her daughter's imminent departure from home were left to her and Bendang had receded into one of his silent phases. Happenings in the big house were also a matter of concern: the old woman was becoming more forgetful, more cantankerous and morose. She complained to relatives and visitors that no one cared for her, that they did not give her enough food, and sometimes she went to the extent of claiming that the servants were trying to poison her. All these complaints would come to Aosenla and she would drop whatever she was doing to rush to her mother-in-law, calm her down, coax her to have a bath and put her to sleep. 'I am looking after three children,' she would think, and would correct herself immediately, 'no, not three, but four!' adding Bendang to the list.

These domestic concerns bothered her but she was able to deal with them. It was really the unarticulated fear about the little girl's presence in Kilang's Home that plunged her into dark depression. As time went on, she began to blame herself for this turn of events. Why hadn't she refused to have anything to do with the baby? Why did she involve Kilang at all, making him an accomplice in the cover-up while at the same time ensuring that she had minimum contact with him on a one-to-one basis? Was this what her husband and Kilang had discussed that night? What would she do if the truth were known? What would happen to her daughters? And what would happen to the unspoken sympathy she detected in Kilang's attitude towards her from time to time? Was he already blaming her for this and was this what had driven him to talk to Bendang? Though outwardly she was behaving like a loving mother, a caring wife and a dutiful daughter-in-law for the entire world to see, the real Aosenla was once again assailed by doubt and would often seek quiet places in her surroundings to keep her anxieties under control.

During the rare moments of quietude, she began to realize that she was losing control over her life and that past events were starting to overwhelm the neat little world that she had built around her daughters. Despite occasional moments of inner disquiet, she had been content with the seemingly even tenor of her life, until this little orphan appeared out of nowhere and threatened to overturn their well-ordered lives. Not only that, but she had, out of sheer desperation, entangled the good doctor in the mess created by Bendang in his youth. Aosenla constantly dreaded the consequences of the exposure of Tiajungla's origins and her presence in the Home.

24

One day Kilang presented himself at her doorstep without any advance notice. Aosenla thought that the end of the game was at hand and stepped back as if she was looking at an apparition instead of at the family doctor. Kilang was surprised by her reaction and did not know what to do or say. Deciding that it was a bad time, he turned to walk away but Aosenla's stopped him, 'Doctor, if you walk away, I'll never speak to you again.' He was now thoroughly confused; what had he done or said that she should behave like this? Where were her manners, this woman who was always so polite, calm and composed no matter what the situation? Still in a daze and without saying a word, he retraced his steps and entered the living room. Aosenla closed the door and, asking him to sit, took a corner chair herself. They sat in silence for a while, then Kilang spoke; 'I came to meet you because I have some good news.' At this her face changed, she looked somewhat relieved. He continued, 'Remember, you asked me not to advertise the adoption provision for Tiajungla? I kept my promise to you, but someone came to me the other day and asked for her by name. When I told her that the child's adoption was still not decided, she accused me of being dishonest and asked me if I was ready to face the consequences if I tried to block the adoption. It was a veiled threat, which made me think that she knew the truth about this child's parentage. She insisted that I produce the adoption papers and when I resisted, she left in a huff saying that I had a week's time to complete the formalities after which she would find "other means" to take the baby away.' As she listened to the account of this mysterious visitor's demand, Aosenla realized that this woman could be a close relative of the child. Then a wild thought came to her. Could she be the grandmother, the woman who was abandoned by Bendang so callously decades ago? 'Who is this woman?' she asked Kilang. He said he did not know because she refused to give her name. He remembered that she brushed aside his query and simply said, 'None of your business now but you will see it in the papers.' 'But,' he continued, 'she was confident and said that she would take the baby, by force if need be.' So he had come to Aosenla to discuss this and said that it would be good for all concerned if the baby was given for adoption without any fuss, and within the week as the angry woman had demanded.

The worried look came back and Aosenla looked at him for a long time before finally mustering enough courage to ask him, 'Was this what you discussed with my husband the other evening?' Kilang was puzzled at first and did not say anything. 'Tell me,' urged Aosenla, 'I'll not be angry with you; after all it is my fault that I dragged you into this mess.' This time it was Kilang who stared at her and answered in a calm voice, 'Madam, what I discussed with your husband has nothing to do with the baby and I am surprised that you should think that I would betray your trust in this manner.' Aosenla was immensely relieved but also ashamed that she had doubted his integrity. She simply said, 'I am terribly sorry Doctor, for hurting your sentiments but you know that there is a lot on my mind these days and often I cannot think straight.' At this Kilang seemed to relent and replied simply, 'I understand madam, don't worry about my feelings. But we have to decide about the adoption, so can you please come to the clinic tomorrow in the first hour if possible?' Without waiting for her reply, he quietly walked out.

After the doctor's departure, Aosenla sat alone in the room for a while and only when a servant from the big house came looking for her, she stirred out of her meditation and went to see what the old woman had done this time. It turned out to be one of those days when her mother-in-law had decided to shout loudly that her house was on fire and start throwing things out of her room. She was ordering the servants to bring water to douse the fire and would soon begin jumping up and down the corridor, stark naked. Aosenla knew the pattern. Fortunately, today the servant had fetched her before the old lady could get rid of her clothes. On such days, she would ask for a wet towel which she would press against the old woman's eyes and say, 'There, there, the fire is out but let us go out for some fresh air, the house is still smoky.' With that ploy she would bring her to her own house where she would settle her into a sofa and put the television on. The sounds from the machine would immediately make the old woman look at the screen and, gazing intently on the figures, she would soon fall asleep after the exertions of fighting the imagined fire.

It had been, on the whole, a hectic day and Aosenla felt totally drained. But she had to think over the adoption issue and come to a decision. Otherwise, the nameless woman might jeopardize what little peace she had enjoyed. The more she thought about it, the more convinced she became that letting the baby go was the best way. But why was she feeling a pang at the prospect? What was the baby to her? Wasn't she, for all purposes, the living reminder of Bendang's dark deed and a threat to her daughters' happiness? She could not understand her own reaction to the idea of Tiajungla not being a part of her world. Somewhere in her mind she had started associating this little girl's situation with her own; an absurd proposition, she often chided herself. But the utter helplessness of the orphan had struck a familiar chord in her mind, reminding her of her own sense of being utterly alone even now within a seemingly ideal marriage. And now she was facing the prospect of losing all contact with the one human being whom she had considered a fellow sufferer. Though the fact remained that the existence of this little girl was a stark symbol of Bendang's heartless cruelty, Aosenla somehow could not turn her disgust on to the orphan. Instead, she viewed her with a deep sympathy, which extended to the abandoned mother as well. And also perhaps with a mother's instinct to preserve a child, any child, she had lately begun to fantasize about giving this waif all her love and somehow finding a good home for her in the town so that she could quietly keep a watch on her. But now that the prospect of a stranger taking her away became more or less a certainty, this dealt a heavy blow to Aosenla's sensitive soul. But she was also aware that if she interfered in any way, Bendang would become suspicious. She could not afford to upset the equilibrium of their relationship because she knew deep in her heart that should anything tip that balance, she and her daughters would be the real victims.

So after a troubled night of tossing and turning, during which her husband slept peacefully, Aosenla woke up with a new resolve. She would not deviate from her priorities and would keep the welfare of her 'world', a world she had created with so much discipline and calculation, as her one and only priority. The decision taken, she became more animated and decisive in her actions. She gave instructions to her servants, went to the big house to see to her mother-in-law's needs and after satisfying herself that everything was in order in both the houses, she got ready and went to meet Kilang about the adoption papers for Tiajungla. Kilang was waiting for her and after she went through the old grandfather's permission slip and made sure that the identity of the girl's parents was not on any document, Aosenla said goodbye to the doctor and got in the car to go home. As she turned out of the gates of the Home, another car drew in, and Aosenla saw the woman in the back staring at her intently. Something in that focused glare alerted Aosenla and she wondered for a moment if this was the woman who had abandoned her own daughter and was now trying to expiate her guilt by trying to adopt the granddaughter. But it was too short a glance and Aosenla could not glean anything from the brief sighting; she only said a silent prayer for Tiajungla, the orphan girl she had given the name to with so much love and hope.

She came home in a despondent mood and retired early. Bendang was away at a meeting and she knew that he would be back late. Her rational self told her to let go of even the memory of the child. But her heart would not let her rest without a last farewell to the little girl she had felt so close to. Ultimately her heart won and she began to plan for a last visit to the Home on some pretext or the other where she could learn more about Tiajungla's future. This time around, she enlisted the help of her faithful maid and sent her on a secret errand to Kilang because she did not want to become conspicuous by her frequent visits to the Home, especially now when she knew that the other workers there would also have learnt about the adoption issue. The maid carried a bundle of new baby clothes ostensibly from the women's group of which Aosenla was the President. But she also asked Kilang to come to the house the next day because Bendang had gone off to see his friend Dr Bora in Jorhat.

Kilang did not come on the appointed day and Aosenla

began to panic; had something gone wrong? Was the child sick, or worse still, was the other woman demanding full details of the child's antecedents? She spent the entire day wandering around the house and gardens in a distracted fashion, eating only when her maid brought her meal to her room. The next day, she woke up with a dreadful headache and feared the worst: either her husband would suddenly come back when Kilang was with her or the doctor would never appear at all. After a while, she composed herself and took a leisurely bath and got dressed. She called the maid and asked her to get ready too as they were going to the market. Just as the maid was going out, she heard a car turn into her compound and there he was, the much-awaited doctor. Aosenla hurriedly dismissed her maid and, composing herself, tried to be as calm as she could. Once in the drawing room, she waited for Kilang to begin the 'meeting'. On his part, the doctor did not know how to begin the conversation, though he had guessed, as soon as he received her message, that there could be only one reason why she wanted to meet him during her husband's absence.

Then he began to speak. 'Madam, I'm sorry that I could not come yesterday as the whole day was taken up by Tiajungla's adoption and I am happy to inform you that everything went off as you wanted. As a matter of fact, there was nothing I could have done to prevent the adoption because the lady who came to me was well-informed about the circumstances of the baby's entry to my Home and....' At this juncture Aosenla intervened, 'How? And who is she?' Kilang paused for a moment and said, 'Maybe I should begin with the lady: she is a practising lawyer from Jorhat and has been hired by Ajungla's grandmother.' Aosenla said, 'But how did she know? She had cut off all her ties with her family. Tell me who told her about Tiajungla's existence and where to find her? Did anyone from your Home inform her?

But how? No one was told who her parents or grandparents were.' Seeing her obvious distress over the possible betrayal by someone close to them, Kilang once again took up his interrupted narrative about how the lawyer came to his Home asking specifically for the orphan named Tiajungla.

'I did not welcome the lady's enquiries at first and tried to be evasive about Ajungla's antecedents, even adding that we never allowed babies from the Home to be adopted by people from out of town. Besides, I remembered your wish to keep the adoption clause from public knowledge for some more time, and so I acted accordingly; but to no avail, because this lawyer lady had come armed with sworn affidavits from the old man himself giving all the details about the birth and the eventual lodging of his unfortunate great-granddaughter in my Home.' 'But how?' Aosenla asked. 'It seems,' Kilang continued, 'after he went to the village the old man kept on dreaming about Tiajungla's mother, his granddaughter. He felt she was cursing him and accusing him of giving up the child to 'strangers' and demanding that he bring her back to her. He dismissed the dreams at first, but then he began to think that he heard her cries in the daytime too, at home or even in the fields where he went when he could not bear the atmosphere at home. So eventually one day he sat down and wrote a very difficult letter to his estranged daughter giving all the details of the little girl's birth and where to find her if she wanted to see her. Madam, I want to assure you that no one from my establishment knows about this and it will remain so, because even the lawyer wanted to keep it that way to protect her client's own family from the long-ago scandal. Of course Tiajungla will grow up in her household but only as an adopted child and their relationship will remain a secret forever, I hope,' he added. 'But madam, I did something of my own volition and I hope you will not be angry with me.' 'What is it?' Aosenla asked, 'I made a condition for the adoption, I told the lady that the name Tiajungla must always be a part of this girl's name, even if they wanted to give her another name. And to this she readily agreed saying that it was a beautiful name and remarked that there could be no better name for a child like this because she was now going to have a very good fate and future.'

As she sat listening to Kilang's account of the mapping of Tiajungla's future, Aosenla began to feel a strange emotion inside her; earlier she had had doubts about Kilang's loyalty, and had wondered what would happen to her marriage if the secret of Tiajungla's birth were to become known. But now, instead of relief she felt only an inexplicable emptiness, as if a vital cord of her inner being had been snapped off. She also felt that at that moment she could have made Kilang do anything she wanted. But the sedate housewife came to the fore and began to pour out the tea that her maid had brought for them. While sipping the welcome brew, she congratulated the doctor for completing the adoption issue so successfully and added, 'You know Doctor, I chose the name Tiajungla for the little girl because I believed that she had a good destiny and I am extremely grateful to you because you too endorsed this. Thank you once more for everything you have done for her.' Kilang thought that she had said her last word and was about to get up when he saw that she was struggling to say something more. So he waited. After what appeared to be a heroic effort to keep her tears at bay, Aosenla blurted out, 'Kilang, I cannot even begin to tell you what my life would have been if you were not around to support me and help me out of very difficult and dangerous situations. I will ever cherish your goodwill. Yet forgive me if I seem ungrateful or indifferent for saying this; but now I must return to my destined routine and so must you; believe me I know it is best this way. But let us always remain friends.' And without waiting for a response from the bewildered man, she touched his hand ever so lightly and quickly went inside.

On his way home from this unusual encounter, the doctor suddenly realized that through all the years of his association with the family, Aosenla had never even once called him by his first name and he slowly began to understand that it was her way of telling him that she was not insensitive or unaware of his feelings for her. And maybe, he thought, she was trying to convey her reciprocation by taking his first name in the intimacy of a private meeting. But deep in his heart he knew that the acknowledgement was also a termination; a termination of the bond that had drawn them closer, sometimes dangerously close. But Aosenla's last decisive words, 'let us always remain friends,' more or less restored the social status quo and ensured that both of them remained 'safe'.

No one would have suspected that an upright citizen like Kilang, a devoted husband and father and a practising Christian who had dedicated his life to helping the poor and needy, would have any feelings for another woman, that too, a married one and above all, one who belonged to one of the most prominent families of the town. Back at home he closeted himself in his tiny office and began to introspect. In the sanctuary of his room, where his wife seldom visited, he tried to reconstruct the events which had created this convoluted network involving him, Bendang and Aosenla. He did not realize how tired he was and closed his eyes for a minute which stretched into a deep slumber of almost an hour. When he awoke from this much-needed rest, he felt fresh and began to assess the events with a clearer head and concluded that whatever the fallout of his association with the couple, the one undeniable factor was that he responded to their call for help every time a crisis loomed over the family.

For quite a while he sat there feeling a vague sense of resentment, mainly against Aosenla, who seemed to him to be the key manipulator. But deep in his mind he also knew that he had developed a grudging sense of admiration for this woman. Though he knew that tonight's final words from her were a form of dismissal, he could not help wondering what would have happened if she had not emerged the stronger of the two and assumed the role of the decider. This realization helped him understand why she was successful in building a seemingly normal life with a person like Bendang.

Back in her room, Aosenla was overtaken by an immense fatigue, both of mind and body. Stretching out on the big bed, she began to think of that disastrous moment when her maid had blurted out the truth about the birth of Bendang's illegitimate granddaughter. And when she thought back on the chain of events which were put in motion solely by her diktats, she was amazed at her own actions; how adroitly she had manipulated the circumstances and how concerned and protective she had become of this child: and she remembered how at that panic-laden moment Kilang was the only person she could turn to. This child, disowned and virtually abandoned by those closest to her, had thus become the agent through which her association with Kilang had assumed different contours. Now that the need for secrecy had gone, almost as though through divine intervention, she admitted to herself that she and Kilang had truly been treading on quicksand and shuddered to think of how close she had been to dismantling her well-constructed world of social propriety. But it gave her no joy to think of this 'liberation' via the exit of this threatening agent. Inwardly she grieved and felt that a beautiful interlude in her life had come to an end.

The unobtrusive departure of Tiajungla from a well-ordered society in a small town went unnoticed and un-felt by most of the actors in this drama. It was in such sharp contrast to the little girl's appearance almost at her doorstep that Aosenla found it anti-climatic. The two people most intimately involved in the dramatic events of Tiajungla's brief sojourn with them, Aosenla and Kilang, quietly joined the ranks of the unknowing because they now realized that to have done otherwise would have served no purpose. It was like a sudden storm that had invaded their staid lives. Now that the little girl had gone, and the shadow of her existence no longer loomed over them, they could breathe easy. Years later, they would wonder about the little girl and hope that in some small way, they had helped launch her into a better life.

25

In the meantime the ordered lives of the two main actors continued more or less in the same tempo, neither of them overstepping the line of propriety in word or deed. Bendang often wondered how the doctor overcame his financial problems, but he kept his own counsel even when the townspeople started talking that some foreigners were donating money for the Home. And sure enough, after about two and a half years, a new building on his vacant plot came up, which they said was going to be a Home for the Aged. The local population was eager to see at least some of these 'foreign' benefactors but what 'foreigners' they saw coming to the Home once in a while, all looked, according to them, 'like Madrasis'!

Nothing seemed to have changed in the two houses where Aosenla was now the undisputed mistress, her mother-in-law having passed away after a brief illness. On balmy afternoons, she would sit out on the verandah of her own house and look benignly on the big one. Where once she saw threatening presences, now only shadows from overgrown trees played hide-and-seek. 'We have to do something about the big house,' she once told her husband after the old woman died. Bendang shrugged and said, 'Do what you think best,' and they left it at that for more than a year. The servants in the old house had been sent away, some weeping, but some others relieved to be free of the tyranny of the old woman. The house itself began to lose its aura, being left untended for long. The paint faded and the roof started leaking in some places. The compound too began to look like a jungle, flowering bushes grew into shaggy trees and creepers overshot their trellises into all available spaces, giving the huge structure and its surrounding space an almost gothic appearance. Still Aosenla did not lift a finger to remove the veritable disgrace growing uglier by the day, right beside her trim little cottage. It was as if she was gloating over the decay and destruction of the 'Big House'. As time went on, she no longer bothered to look at it as she sat on her verandah reading letters from her daughters.

One day as Aosenla sat in her favourite corner of the verandah ruminating over the events of the past years, she happened to glance at the ugly mass that the big house had become and she sat up with a loud gasp, asking herself 'What's happening to me? Why have I become so indifferent to life around me?' It was as if the ugliness proliferating right under her nose was pointing a finger at her and blaming her for what she had allowed to happen to the once imposing compound. She felt guilty and became restless: calling loudly for her old gardener, she ran ahead to the front porch of the other house. She found it littered with bird shit, fallen leaves and even some dead birds. She screamed for all the servants and ordered them to clean the porch and asked the gardener to engage some labourers to clear the overgrown trees and hedges the very next day. This sudden spurt of activity seemed to energize her in a strange way. It made her feel that she was doing something worthwhile after a very long time. Somehow she felt that she had regained the control that she had let slip through sheer lethargy.

As the surroundings of the big house were being trimmed and cleaned, the inside posed a more challenging task. Paint was peeling off from the walls and ceilings; the fraying upholstery was coated with the dust of long neglect. The furniture was dulled by the encrusted grime and one could not cross the doorways because of the thick network of cobwebs. There were several holes in the tin roof through which rainwater had seeped in and in many places the wooden floor was dangerous to step on. Aosenla remembered how these rotting floors had shone with varnish rigorously applied by the many servants every day. Except for the foundations, everything else about the house was decrepit. As the labourers, headed by the gardener, attacked the overgrowth outside, Aosenla crept from room to room in horrified surprise to gape at the devastation inside. Bendang had refused to have anything to do with the project of renovating the big house, so this tremendous responsibility lay on her shoulders alone and she had to finish what she had so impulsively begun. She was truly astonished to see how decay had set in so fast. Mulling over the enormity of the task, Aosenla entered the master bedroom on the third day of her enterprise. As soon as she set foot in the room, she felt as though the old woman was peering at her from the dirty dusty bed and she instantly remembered the many occasions when she cajoled the almost senile woman to lie down on that bed. She also remembered how her mother-in-law used to prise wads of money from the drawers and offer them to her. She resisted her first impulse to open the drawers, but then she gave in and opened one. It was empty. She went on to the next and found that it contained some shawls now frayed and in tatters which would probably disintegrate into dust at a touch. She closed it with a bang. She decided that she'd done enough snooping for the day; but curiosity pushed her to the one below the bed and she tried to pry it loose. But it would not budge; something was stuck. Bending low and feeling with her hand, she found that a side of the drawer had rotted and the loose strip was preventing it from opening easily. Applying both her hands, she pulled at the handle with all her strength and with the splintering of the remaining boards, the drawer fell to the floor. And in it Aosenla found rolls of currency notes, bound by rubber bands now curling and crumbling when she tried to remove them. She stood up, exhausted by the effort, and kicked the bundles around the room muttering, 'So much for your secret hoarding, you old witch,' and stumbled out of the mouldy room to the sunshine outside.

The restoration of the old house was a job easily done by hired labourers and it took them less than two months to clean, repair and repaint the house. The garden too was beginning to look alive and trim, being tended by the expert hands of the old gardener's son. The big house almost looked as majestic as it used to in the days when her mother-in-law was its dreaded mistress. But only Aosenla knew that something vital had disappeared from it because it no longer intimidated her. She had seen the devastation time can inflict not only on human lives but on the things human beings own. Comparing her own demure cottage standing strong and resolute by the once formidable presence of the big house, Aosenla realized that outward appearances can be so misleading. Her mother-in-law, basking in the aura of her husband and her position as the matriarch of a formidable family, had seemed absolutely invincible; but she had witnessed how helpless and vulnerable she had become once the protective power of her husband was snatched away from her. She wondered if the same would happen to her too if Bendang were to die before her. But instantly she pulled herself up and muttered, 'Stop this nonsense, don't think such morbid thoughts,' and she turned her attention to her own household. But there was a deep conviction within her that she would never feel or act as the old woman had.

The restoration had a cathartic effect on Aosenla; she marvelled at the expert way the workers had tackled each aspect, how they tried to blend the new fittings to match the old ones so that when the paint was finally applied, the distinction between the two seemed to disappear. The ultimate result was that it was the old house, but at the same time she knew that it was not the same old house. At first it amused her, this metamorphosis of an inanimate thing that had held such power over her. Such musings began to turn her thoughts inwards and on many afternoons as she sat on her own verandah in clear view of the other house, she began to look back on her life from the moment she entered this big compound to begin her life as its much sought-after daughter-in-law. But she also knew that she was resented for being what she was: an insignificant girl of poor parentage brought into the prestigious family because of her pedigree. Those were moments when she would ask herself if she was the same Aosenla who had entered this family as a reluctant bride.

Did anything remain of the timid girl that she had been? The physical self of that girl was no longer there of course; but what about the inner self? And had she really 'owned' that self ever? Who or what had she become now? Every time she sat in her verandah and looked at the old house, now no longer with dread, but rather with a sense of triumph, she wondered, was she the one responsible for the transition? How much say had she really had in her own life and the affairs of her family?

The most difficult of all the questions continued to be this: what had she been trying to achieve in her life? Apart from all the apparent demands on her as a wife, mother, daughter-in-law and a society lady, what was happening to her inner self? Did she not adjust her many different selves according to the demands and expectations of others? And in doing so, had she forgotten something essential about herself? If she were to 'own' a single self, which one would it be?

These perplexing questions come and go but on many a pleasant evening one can see a middle-aged woman with grey streaks in her hair sitting on the verandah of a neat cottage, gazing intently on a newly painted house within the same compound. No one can say what her thoughts are during these pensive moments. Sometimes she chuckles over what appears to be a letter here and a newspaper there; sometimes she calls for the gardener to discuss the season's flowers and vegetables. Most times she prefers to be left alone. Sometimes she snores rather loudly, her dishevelled hair fluttering in the breeze of the overhead fan. None of the servants dares disturb her, even when it becomes dark. She will emerge in her own time from the recesses of her mind where she is trying to find answers to many questions, chief among which is: who she really is. Is she Aosenla, the reluctant bride and the timid wife, or the disappointing daughter-in-law who could not produce a male heir for the big house? Or is she the wife who once craved for her husband's approval and love but no longer cared if he loved her or not? She wonders if she is now the amalgamated self of all these other selves and often thinks that she would like to be free of these imposed selves, which have grown on her unawares over the years. But then, she asks, who would she be without them? She would be stripped bare of the only acceptable persona she has become by suppressing her real self, the essential Aosenla. Does this mean she has been diminished in some way?

When she stirs and goes into the house, she becomes Aosenla, the mistress of her own little world where her authority is absolute. Is this what she has become, just another matriarch lording it over a petty, limited sphere?

Where have the dreams gone? Where is that Aosenla who had once wanted to chart her own destiny? Where is that Aosenla who had once tried to entice her husband into the circle of her love through her body? Where has that love gone? Is she now even capable of another kind of love? And then it strikes her that it is the vital 'absence' of this one fundamental element in the marriage that has stunted her whole life. Because of this, there was always an empty place in her heart throughout these years. But it is amazing that it no longer bothers her at all. She had also realized that because of the absence of any strong emotional bond between her and her husband she has actually been able to tolerate her position in the marital equation. She has understood that she has remained a mere 'possession' to her husband all along, but even this does not trouble her anymore. But there persists a most disturbing question in her mind: has she allowed herself to be 'made over' like the old house, to become what others want her to be? Has she betrayed herself by abandoning her own self?

The image of the restored house impinges on Aosenla's thinking as she continues to sit in the verandah day after day. And then one day an amazing idea comes to her: she is like the old house! Whatever has happened outwardly to it, the old house stands on its original site as though guarding an inner essence. She takes comfort in this thought and mulls over it. The big house had been more than just a house to her; it had symbolized authority and invincibility. But now, she reasons, if even such a symbol could be ravaged and its significance diffused by time, who was she to think that she, the frail girl called Aosenla, could remain untouched by the environment around her? And just like the old house has held on to its identity, she tells herself that despite all the upheavals, she has not betrayed nor relinquished her original self. She is that essential Aosenla to herself and she will always remain true to herself. But she also begins to understand that no one entirely and absolutely owns one's self because that self has to exist within a given circumstance, and the moment she accepts this, she seems to have entered another space in her life. She is released.

Every day now, the hair grows greyer, the body more lethargic and she no longer cares about the garden or what is happening in her kitchen. She sits alone in the verandah turning to the inner turmoils of her mind, asking unanswerable questions about who she has become. Once in a while, her husband of many years ambles out to join her in wordless companionship in the dying hours of the day. Occasionally a letter flutters to the ground, which he picks up to show her. She gestures to tell him she's read it. He glances over it and sometimes wordlessly totters back into the warmth of his study, but most days he simply reclines in the armchair and ruminates and recalls the minutest details of the day.

For example, Aosenla's wordless gesture that afternoon, telling him that she had read the letter that he picked up from the floor to show her, was the kind of non-communication that they inflicted on each other. He thinks sadly: these are the little indications of how he and his wife have drifted apart in their declining years, though each tries to create a cordiality which might fool casual observers. The funny thing is, they both know what the other is trying to do. Though he is not a person capable of deep introspection, Bendang has studied the varied moods of his wife through the years and is still wary of her whims. The most important question on his mind lately has been: had he ever entertained anything called 'love' for his wife? At times he wonders, 'Is this what love is?' In his own way, the seemingly introverted, almost cold person is relinquishing the negativity of his inner self and is undergoing a subtle change to come to terms with life as it is now. He is also hoping that there will be a time when he will be able to come closer to the woman whom he has taken for granted for so long.

Then one day it happens: there is bewilderment in her eyes as she reads the day's letter: it is from her daughter Chubala announcing to her parents that she is planning to introduce her boyfriend to them during the winter break when she comes home. She adds that he is a fellow doctor and comes from a good family, subtly implying that the parents will surely approve of her choice. She does not mention his name or who his parents are. But she stresses on the fact that as far as they are concerned they considered themselves 'engaged' because they were friends from their second year onwards, and she hopes that her parents will also accept her decision to marry him.

Aosenla is at first overjoyed at the news but she pauses and begins to think: when did her daughter tell them that she had a boyfriend? And almost engaged? Did she ask them for permission? Why did she not mention his name and who his people are? Are they Christians or Hindus? She begins to seethe inwardly; the cheek of this girl trying to foist this stranger on them and suggesting that he is going to be their son-in-law! Aosenla feels that she is caught in a trap, the trap of time. She sits there numbed by this bombshell. What are they going to do? She gets up slowly and ambles into the house calling out loudly to her husband, 'Bendang, Bendang, come out and read this. Where are you old man, come and read what your daughter has written.'

There is a faint shuffle near the door and Bendang comes out with his thick glasses on, as if to lose no time in reading his daughter's letter. As he sits down, Aosenla thrusts the letter at him. He reads attentively and only sighs. The wife glares at him and almost screams, 'What, you've nothing to say? Do you know who this boy is?' He looks up at his irate wife and takes her hands in his. She snatches them back as if his touch has scorched her and gives him such a look that the smile fades from his face. But determined not to be cowed down, he valiantly produces a smile again, 'No, I don't know who he is or who his people are. But of one thing I am sure: if Chubala has chosen him, I will accept him as my son-in-law. You know Asen, times have changed and we must accept the fact that our children are not like us and will never be so. Please try to understand that today we live in a different world.'

Aosenla sits down slowly, almost reluctantly, speechless and totally baffled by the words she has just heard. When and how did this transformation in her husband happen? Instead of trying to exercise his will as the father, he is allowing his daughter to make her own decision! And about such a serious matter as marriage? And then suddenly Aosenla becomes pensive once more and she retires to her bedroom and locks the door. In the privacy of her sanctuary she recalls her own marriage where she was never consulted or listened to; it happened because her father wished it to happen. And here is a situation where the father is allying with his daughter!

She feels left out of things once more. But a voice inside her asks, shouldn't she be happy for her daughter? Did she not long for even a bit of understanding from her parents about the marriage that was being thrust upon her? The father was adamant; but what about her own mother? Did she try to plead for her daughter's wishes? Because of her mother's apparent betrayal, Aosenla always entertained a secret grudge against her for letting her down. Is she now doing the same thing? She finds herself in an impossible situation. Her husband's decisive words echo in her mind: 'But of one thing I am sure: if Chubala has chosen him, I will accept him as my son-in-law.' And there she is, fuming at not being consulted or even asked for her approval, and expecting her husband to stand by her. Instead, he is playing the modern, liberated male. Doubly slighted by her husband's attitude, she gets up abruptly and comes out of the room. Bendang knows that there is going to be a storm tonight in the bedroom and asks for his tea in the verandah, with the intention of delaying the inevitable.

The storm comes in the form of banishment. For two days Aosenla sulks and refuses to eat. She has taken to her bed and sends Bendang's essential night things to the guest room. He roams the compound like an abandoned dog and eats his meals in his temporary room. There is an air of doom over the entire household. Even the servants are puzzled and have become gloomy. Bendang does not know what he should do or how he should handle his wife's anger. Anger? He suddenly asks himself. At whom and why? He shakes his head in frustration and resigns himself to more days of silence and bitterness between the two of them.

And then fate intervenes in his favour. On the third day there is message for Bendang that a delegation of some elders of the town wants to meet him. When the party arrives, he is surprised to see Kilang among them. After seating them in the drawing room he goes to request Aosenla to join them. Reluctantly and with a long face Aosenla joins the assembled guests; she greets Kilang in a half-hearted manner. Then an elderly man, who introduces himself as Kilang's cousin, starts to speak: 'Dear Bendang and Asenla, our families have known each other for a long time and therefore let me come straight to the point. We are here today to ask for the hand of your elder daughter Chubala for my son Imliakhum. You may be aware that they know each other well as they studied in the same medical college and have both finished their MBBS exam, and will soon come home for the winter holidays. I believe that your daughter has already written to you about this. There is a special request however: if our offer is accepted, we want the marriage to take place without much delay. You see my wife is not keeping well and it is her desire that the marriage take place soon.' There is a stunned silence; no preamble, no lengthy elaboration of clans and family history as is the custom in such matters but only the blunt proposal and request for an early marriage. Bendang looks at Aosenla as though asking her a question; she simply stares at him. Taking that as a possible rejection from her, Bendang gets up from the chair and thanks the boy's family, saying he and his wife are honoured and that they have to have a family consultation and will let them know as soon as they can. After tea and snacks, the delegation departs, reiterating their offer and requesting them not to take too long to convey their answer.

Aosenla is the first to leave without saying a word. She heads towards the bedroom. Bendang wants to follow her but does not do so, thinking that she needs some time to cool down. But the next day he decides to have it out with her and asks her to come to the verandah. However, when they are seated it is Aosenla who breaks the silence. 'Bendang, I am sorry for what I have done these past days. I realize that I have been mean and unreasonable. Let us be happy for Chubala's sake because I know that she has made the right choice and I can't wait to meet him. Please forgive me but remember that he is going to be our son-in-law, not only yours!' So saying, she begins to weep and laugh at the same time. Bendang looks at this woman he has married. He had wondered when her tirade would begin. But there's a total anti-climax; she is calm and chatty and begins to talk excitedly about the impending wedding in the family and is already making up the guest list! He gets up with a new purpose and goes and puts his arms around his wife, something he has not done in a long while and never in public. Aosenla becomes misty-eyed once more but before she can say or do anything, he quietly retreats to their bedroom, because he knows that he is now reinstated in her scheme of things. As he leaves her, he simply says, 'I'll send our acceptance through my brother-in-law the day after tomorrow. That way we won't appear to be too eager, don't you think?'

During the following days, while both families wait to finalize things, Aosenla often retreats to the verandah and reclines in the easy chair and thinks about their life. She has not forgotten that this marriage will mean that Kilang's tenuous connection to the family will continue. But she is no longer afraid because she has long outgrown that self and has entered a different phase in her life. She glances at the big house and smiles. This is Aosenla the mother, rejoicing in the prospect of a new beginning. She has discarded all her resentments against father and daughter and now looks forward to the future. She gets up and marches into the house. There is no indication of the old pain in her knee-joints, nor any hint of the dizziness that plagues her often. She calls out, 'Bendang, where are you, you old man, come out and let us have tea in the verandah.'

As she returns to her chair, the woman who has led an outwardly unspectacular life, almost a held-back life, sighs a happy sigh because she sees a new beginning of mutual love: her daughter's life. She cannot fully comprehend what her daughter must be feeling, for she has never known that feeling in her life. But she thinks of her daughter's happiness as a fair compensation of her own deprivation and is content. After her initial resentment against her husband for defending the daughter's decision, Aosenla also realizes that unlike her father, what Bendang was ensuring was his daughter's happiness. As he comes through the door, Aosenla sees the slight smile on his face and greets him with one of her own wondering, 'Is this really the man I was forced to marry?' When the tea things are brought, Bendang notices that the maid has laid out one of their best sets and that the linen also looks freshly laundered. He instinctively relaxes and looking at his wife's face radiating calm, thinks, 'Ah! This is the woman I married, but where was she hiding all this time?'

Aosenla might one day realize that her search for her true self has, ironically, been a long process of subversion of that self by the circumstances around her. But now that there is a new understanding not only of herself but also her husband's love and concern for their daughter, a fine balance emerges within the relationship between them. She is free from her earlier insecurities and doubts. She is no longer concerned about who or what she has become. She is at last at ease, with not only herself but with her husband. She is content.